"Mia James?" Bob Taylor, the CEO Alessandro had hired, sounded surprised when he mentioned her. "She's on maternity leave. She had a baby three months ago. A little girl."

For a second Alessandro couldn't speak. Couldn't think. He felt as if his brain were short-circuiting, misfiring. A baby. A baby three months ago...nine months after their night together.

It was impossible. Impossible. She'd been on the pill. She would have told him. It couldn't be...

"Right, I must have forgotten that." His voice, attempting cheer, sounded forced.

"I hope she comes back," Taylor said. "She's a good PA. The best I've ever had."

"Yes." Alessandro's mind felt as if it were buzzing, full of static and white noise. He could not form a single coherent thought. "Yes," he said again, and then he disconnected the call.

Mia James might have had his baby and not even told him. Unless it wasn't his child? A little girl. His mind raced as he paced the confines of the room like something caged. Could it be another man's? Yet she'd been a virgin. Surely it was his. Surely...

There was only one way to find out.

Secret Heirs of Billionaires

There are some things money can't buy...

Living life at lightning pace, these magnates are no strangers to stakes at their highest. It seems they've got it all... That is, until they find out that there's an unplanned item to add to their list of accomplishments!

Achieved:

1. Successful business empire.

2. Beautiful women in their bed.

3. *An heir to bear their name?*

Though every billionaire needs to leave his legacy in safe hands, discovering a secret heir shakes up the carefully orchestrated plan in more ways than one!

Uncover their secrets in:

The Maid's Spanish Secret by Dani Collins

Sheikh's Royal Baby Revelation by Annie West

Cinderella's Scandalous Secret by Melanie Milburne

Unwrapping the Innocent's Secret by Caitlin Crews

Proof of Their One-Night Passion by Louise Fuller

Look out for more stories in the Secret Heirs of Billionaires series coming soon!

Kate Hewitt

THE ITALIAN'S
UNEXPECTED BABY

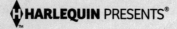 HARLEQUIN PRESENTS®

Recycling programs
for this product may
not exist in your area.

ISBN-13: 978-1-335-14817-9

The Italian's Unexpected Baby

First North American publication 2019

Copyright © 2019 by Kate Hewitt

Printed in U.S.A.

After spending three years as a die-hard New Yorker, **Kate Hewitt** now lives in a small village in the English Lake District with her husband, their five children and a golden retriever. In addition to writing intensely emotional stories, she loves reading, baking and playing chess with her son—she has yet to win against him, but she continues to try. Learn more about Kate at kate-hewitt.com.

CHAPTER ONE

'HE'S COMING!'

Mia James's stomach clenched unpleasantly as she hurried to stand behind her desk, shoulders back, chin up, heart pounding.

'He's in the lift now...'

The numbers above the silver doors glowed, one after another. *Two...three...*

Mia watched out of the corner of her eye as her fellow colleagues at Dillard Investments did the same as she had, scurrying to desks, standing up straight. They were like schoolchildren awaiting an inspection by the head teacher. A particularly strict and perhaps even cruel head teacher...the notoriously ruthless Alessandro Costa, self-made billionaire and, as of yesterday, the new CEO of Dillard Investments.

Yesterday the company had been taken over by Alessandro Costa in a calculated and clever manoeuvre that had shocked everyone involved in the company right down to their toes, including Mia's boss and the CEO, Henry Dillard. Poor Henry had looked terribly shaken, aging ten years in a matter of minutes as he realised there was nothing he could do to stop Costa International from gaining controlling shares; it had all happened before he'd even had a chance to realise, Costa stalking the company the way a ruthless predator would a prey.

Four...five... The lift doors pinged open and Mia drew her breath sharply as the new CEO of Dillard Investments stepped through them. She'd seen photos of him online, having done an exhaustive internet search last night when the news had been confirmed that Dillard's had been taken over. What she'd learned had far from reassured her.

Alessandro Costa specialised in hostile takeovers and then stripping the companies of their assets and employees, to be absorbed into his behemoth of a corporation, Costa International.

A few months ago, he'd taken over a company similar to Dillard's—small, family-owned, a bit antiquated. Now it was virtually gone, swallowed up by the man who was striding onto the top floor of the building Dillard's owned in Mayfair.

Mia tried not to make eye contact with Alessandro Costa, but she found she couldn't stop looking at him. The photos on the internet didn't do him justice, she realised with an uneasy pang of physical awareness. They didn't communicate his intense energy, as if a force field surrounded him, as if he *crackled*.

Cropped dark hair, as black as midnight, framed a face that was all angles and hard lines, from his jaw to his nose to the dark slashes of brows over cold, steel-grey eyes. His body, tall and lethally powerful, was encased in a hand-tailored suit of dark grey silk, the silver tie at his throat matching the colour of his eyes. He made Mia think of a laser, or a sword…something powerful and lethal. *A weapon.*

He came onto the floor with its open-plan desks with quick, purposeful strides, his narrowed, hawk-like gaze moving in quick yet thorough assessment around the room, pinning people in place. It felt as if the very air trembled. Mia was afraid she did. Alessandro Costa was incredibly intimidating.

She knew everyone's job was up for grabs, and most likely down the drain as well. In his last takeover, it had been rumoured that Costa had kept three employees out of forty. As personal assistant to the CEO, Mia knew her position would almost certainly be cut. Costa undoubtedly had his own executive assistant already in place, and as he didn't seem likely to keep Dillard's going as a separate entity, her job had most likely become obsolete last night, with the takeover.

Still, she was determined to try to do *something* to keep it. She'd been working for Dillard Investments since she was nineteen, fresh from a B Tech business course, bright-eyed and determined to make something of herself and, most importantly, to finally be independent.

All her childhood she'd been under the controlling thumb of her unbearably autocratic father, having to do as he said and dance to his tune, however discordant its notes. Her mother had been the same, cringing and hopeful in dispiriting turns, and Mia had vowed to gain her freedom as soon as she could—and never make the same kind of mistake her mother had, by marrying a charming yet controlling man…or any man at all.

So now, while Mia knew she could find another job, she resisted the prospect of being fired from this one for no good reason. She'd been here a long time, had worked hard, and had made a few friends along the way.

She might be likely to lose her job anyway, but she'd go down fighting. She had to, as points of both pride and principle.

Alessandro Costa had stopped in the centre of the room, his feet spread wide, his hands on his hips. He looked like the king of an empire, surveying his domain. Like something out of a fairy tale, except in a three-piece suit.

'Who is Mia James?' he asked, his voice slightly accented, the words crisp and precise as they echoed through the open space.

Mia felt every eye on the floor turn instinctively towards her. Like a child in school being called on by a teacher, she raised her hand, hoping her voice would come out strong.

'I am.' She might have overshot it, she realised; she sounded strident. Aggressive, even, to hide her nervousness.

Alessandro Costa's eyes narrowed even further in appraisal, and his lips flattened into a hard line.

'Come with me,' he said, and walked into Henry Dillard's office, the only private space on the floor, an elegant room with wood panelled walls and leather club chairs, tasteful oil paintings and heavy curtains. It felt like a gentleman's club, or the study of an elegant townhouse, which it very well might once have been. Dillard's offices were in a former home, although much of it had been gutted for desk space.

Costa strode towards the big, mahogany desk, inlaid with leather, that Henry had always sat behind while Mia had taken notes or dictation. Henry had been eccentrically old school; he'd only bought a laptop a few years ago, and he'd still depended on Mia to manage emails and spreadsheets, finding both quite beyond him, and not seeming to mind.

It gave her a pang now to think that was all over; Henry had retreated to his estate in Surrey, and Mia half wondered if she'd ever see him again. Last night, as he'd shuffled out of the office, his business in ruins around him, he'd seemed like an old, broken man, and it had wrung her heart right out. And it was this man's fault.

Alessandro Costa stood behind Henry's old desk, his hands placed flat on its surface, fingers spread wide, as he stared at her, his eyes magnetic, his body radiating barely suppressed energy. Although his expression was focused, it wasn't unfriendly. He looked like a man intent on action, and it made Mia tense, something in her kicking up a notch, ready to respond.

'I need you.' Costa spoke the words matter-of-factly, but stupidly they made Mia's heart skip a silly beat. He didn't mean in *that* way, of course he didn't. But perhaps he meant she might keep her job…

'You…do?'

'Yes, for the moment, at least.' Costa straightened, his gaze surveying her with cool appraisal. 'You've been Dillard's PA for how long?'

'Seven years.'

He nodded slowly. 'And, as far as I can see, you were the plug on his life support.'

Mia blinked, absorbing the cruel bluntness of that statement. 'I wouldn't go that far,' she said quietly, although admittedly there was some truth in it. In reality, Henry Dillard would have been happy playing golf and letting the company his father had founded dwindle away to nothing. The company had been ripe for a takeover, even if he hadn't seen it himself, and Mia had never let herself consider such a possibility.

'Perhaps that's a bit harsh,' Costa allowed, 'but Dillard himself admitted he was behind the times. Of course, many of his clients are, as well.'

'Which begs the question why you took it over,' Mia returned. Costa's eyebrows rose as he kept her gaze, and something sparked to life in Mia, something she most certainly wasn't going to acknowledge.

'Yes, it does, doesn't it?' he remarked. 'Fortunately that is not something you need to concern yourself with.'

And that was her, put firmly in her place. 'Very well.' She met his narrowed, steely gaze unflinchingly, although it cost her. Every time she looked at him she felt something in her spark and tingle in a way she definitely didn't like. The man was intense and a little scary, but there was something that drew her to him as well—something in his fierce energy, his incredible focus. 'So why do you need me?' she asked, deciding that keeping things on track was her best bet.

'I need you because I require your knowledge of

Henry's clients so I can deal with them appropriately. So as long as you prove useful…'

Which sounded like a barely veiled threat, or perhaps just a statement of fact. Mia couldn't imagine Alessandro Costa putting up with anyone who wasn't useful.

'And when I don't prove useful?' she asked, although she had a feeling she didn't want to know the answer.

'Then you'll be let go,' Costa said bluntly. 'I don't keep useless employees. It's bad business practice.'

'What about the rest of the staff?'

'Again, none of your concern.'

Wow. The man had no hesitation in being blunt, yet Mia didn't sense any cruel relish in his words, just simple bare statements of fact, which she could appreciate, even if she didn't like them.

In any case, needlessly sparring with Alessandro Costa was a fast track to being fired, and she wanted to keep her job. She *needed* to keep her job. It felt like the only thing she had.

'All right.' She straightened, tipping her chin up, determined to stay professional and match his focus. 'What would you like me to do?'

Something silver flashed in Alessandro's grey eyes; it almost looked like approval, and it made a ripple of pleased awareness race through her, treacherous and molten, racing through her fingers and down to her toes. 'I want files on all of Dillard's major clients, with notes about any potential quirks, habits, tendencies, or any other pertinent information within the hour. We'll talk through it all then.'

'All right.' Mia thought she could manage that, if only just.

'Good.' Without another word, Alessandro Costa strode out of the office, closing the door firmly behind him.

Mia let out a gusty breath and then, on watery legs, she sank into a chair in front of the desk. Now that he was gone, she realised afresh how much energy Costa drew from her, how much adrenalin he stirred up so her heart still pounded and her head felt light. Talking with him had felt like a full mental and physical workout. Ten minutes of it and she was, strangely, both exhausted and energised.

She was also…affected. The man's forceful personality was only part of his intense charisma; she'd felt as if she couldn't look away from him—the eyes that almost glowed, the barely leashed energy that radiated from him, the power that was evident in every taut line of his body. Even now she breathed in the faint scent of his aftershave, something with sandalwood in it, and she felt the urge to tremble. Thankfully, she didn't.

On still shaky legs Mia rose from her chair. She needed to show Alessandro Costa she was oh-so-useful, and more than that, she was necessary. Essential, even. Because she wasn't ready to contemplate the alternative.

Quickly Mia left Henry's old office and went to her desk immediately outside of it. The crowds that had been waiting for Alessandro Costa's arrival had dispersed, and people were back at their desks, attempting to at least seem as if they were working.

Alessandro was nowhere to be seen, and Mia wondered what he was doing. Inspecting the ranks? *Firing someone?* If the rumours were true, he'd fire most of Dillard's staff, just as he had countless other times, something she couldn't bear to think about. She had to focus. She had a job to do.

Dillard Investments was even more of a sorry mess than he'd realised. After a morning of meeting employees and assessing the company's condition, Alessandro Costa felt nothing but a scathing derision for Henry Dillard, a man whose affable exterior hid a terrible weakness—a weakness that had caused the inevitable loss of his company, his clients' assets, and the well-being of his employees. The man had the appearance of a lovable teddy bear, but Alessandro was glad he'd put an end to his benevolent ineptitude.

By refusing to keep up with the times and seek out new opportunities and investments, Henry Dillard had been slowly, or not so slowly, running his company as well as his clients' portfolios into the red, content to live off his dwindling profits and focus on his golf game. If Alessandro hadn't taken over the company, someone else surely would have.

Better, though, that it was him. This was his field of expertise, after all, and what he'd made his life's mission: taking over failing or corrupt companies and turning them into something useful, or else dismantling them completely.

As Alessandro knew and had seen, over and over again, the opportunity of defeating the enemy lay within the enemy himself...discovering his weaknesses and finding his vulnerabilities. It was a concept from Sun Tzu's *The Art of War*, and what Alessandro had learned long ago was that not only was business war, but *life* was war, a battle fought every day, and he had the scars to prove it. Yes, life was war… And he was in it to win.

At least a third of the employees he'd met with today would have to be fired. It seemed as if Dillard had never let anyone go, whether out of sentimentality, stupidity, or just sheer laziness Alessandro didn't know or particularly care.

He always tried to keep redundancies to a minimum, preferring to transfer people to other positions within his portfolio of companies, but many of the staff he'd met here clearly didn't deserve such an opportunity. Dillard's PA, Mia James, being a notable exception…

Surprisingly, reluctantly, Alessandro had been intrigued by her. She was beautiful in a very boring, very English way—straight blonde hair, cornflower blue eyes, a clear, healthy complexion, a tall and athletic figure, without any noticeable curves. *Competent*… in every way, and not the kind of woman that usually sparked his sensual interest.

She was the kind of woman, Alessandro reflected, who had probably been captain of her hockey team at school, who hiked on weekends and had had crushes on horses rather than boys growing up. Who would marry a suitable man and have the requisite two children, a boy and a girl. No one, clearly, whom he would let himself be interested in, much less pursue.

Yet she'd intrigued him. And he didn't like to be intrigued, especially not by a PA whom he would most likely transfer as soon as possible, because he worked best alone. Always had, always would, in every way possible. That was the only way he knew how to conduct his life, learned in childhood and honed to a highly polished skill in adulthood, and he didn't see it changing. Ever.

Mia James was waiting for him in Dillard's office when he walked in an hour after he'd last seen her, to the minute. Alessandro always kept to time, kept his word. Stayed in control, even in such seemingly small, incidental matters, as a point of principle, a matter of pride.

'Well?' he asked. 'Do you have the files?'

She'd risen from her chair as he'd entered, making him notice, rather unwillingly, her long, slender legs encased in sheer black tights, her feet in low black heels. She wore a black pencil skirt and blazer, a crisp white blouse, a simple gold pendant at her throat. Her long, wheat-coloured hair was caught cleanly behind in a clip. He could not fault anything about her, and yet he still felt discomfited. Irritated, even, by his own interest as much as her presence.

He didn't let people affect him. He didn't *do* emotions, and he most definitely didn't act on them. His own unsettled childhood was testament to the power of emotions, as well as the danger, which was why he behaved in a tightly controlled way that made *sense*. Because Alessandro Costa needed to be in control. Always.

'I have everything right here,' Mia said, her voice calm and cool. Unflappable, unlike how he was feeling, which annoyed him further. 'Personal files and relevant information on Dillard's ten most important clients.'

'And how did you determine they were the most important?' Alessandro asked, his voice something close to a snap.

Her clear blue gaze met his; she seemed untroubled by his tone. 'They are the largest investors, and they've been with Dillard's the longest amount of time.'

'Everyone's been with Dillard's since the time of dinosaurs,' Alessandro returned, his irritation making him more callous than he normally would have let himself be. 'That's the nature of the place.'

'Dillard's longevity is one of its points of pride,' Mia agreed, her voice—and what a low, pleasant voice it was—carefully equable. She would not rise to his irritable bait. Another point in her favour, yet unreasonably this just annoyed him further.

He sprawled in the chair behind the desk, beckoning her forward with one hand. 'So show me.'

Mia hesitated for the barest of seconds—hardly noticeable except Alessandro felt so weirdly attuned to her—and then she scooped up the pile of folders and walked around to his side of the desk, placing them in front of him and then flipping the first one open.

'James Davis, a millionaire who set up his own company to manage his financial interests. Inherited money. Generous to a fault. Affable and easy-going but very little common sense. Happy to follow a lead, generally speaking.'

Alessandro was silent, reluctantly impressed by how quickly and clearly she'd summed up the client. Given him all the relevant information, without anything unnecessary, exactly as he would have wanted. So few people impressed him, but Mia James had. *In more ways than one.*

He glanced down at the top sheet detailing the man's investments but the figures blurred in front of him as he inhaled Mia James's scent—something understated and citrusy. She was standing quite close to him, her breasts on a level with his gaze. Not that he was looking, but he did notice how the crisp white cotton with discreet pin tucks highlighted her trim figure. Perhaps curves were overrated.

What was he thinking?

Now seriously annoyed with himself and his unruly thoughts, Alessandro flipped through the pages, skimming all the relevant details with more focus than usual. 'He's operating at a loss,' he observed after a moment.

'Yes.' Another tiny hesitation. 'Many of Dillard's clients are, in the current financial climate. Henry—Mr Dillard—was confident things would bounce back, or at least even out, in the next eighteen months.'

When he would have been retired, with no need to worry about the financial markets or how they were affecting his clients. Alessandro had spoken to Henry Dillard on the phone yesterday, when the takeover had been complete. He always tried to treat his adversaries with dignity, especially when he'd won, which he always did.

Dillard had been furious to be bested by someone he considered his social inferior—and had made that quite clear. Alessandro had taken it in his stride; it was hardly unusual when he chose to target companies run by men like Henry Dillard—entitled, wealthy, and weak. He almost felt sorry for the man; he hadn't been corrupt, like some of the CEOs Alessandro had taken down, just inept. He'd frittered away his family's company, indifferent to his clients' needs, and now he was angry that someone he didn't think deserved his company had won it fairly. Alessandro had no respect for such people. He'd dealt with too many in his life—first as a child, when he'd had no power, and then as a man, when he'd made sure that he did.

'Eighteen months is a lifetime in the stock market,' he told Mia. 'Henry Dillard should have known that.'

Mia drew a quick breath. 'As I said, longevity—'

'Was one of Dillard's assets. It isn't any more.' He swivelled to face her, tilting his head up to meet her blue, blue eyes. As their gazes met and tangled something clanged inside him, like an almighty bell. He felt it reverberate through his whole body, and he thought Mia did as well, judging from the way her pupils dilated, and she moistened her lips with her tongue.

'Sit down,' he ordered, and surprise flared briefly in her eyes before she complied silently, taking the seat across from him, so the desk was between them.

That was better. Now he wouldn't be distracted. He wouldn't let himself.

'Next, please,' he ordered, and calmly Mia took him through the rest of the clients—all of them old money, with an outdated view of investment, wealth, risk, everything. Dillard Investments was an institution that had lazily rested on its well-worn laurels for far too long…which was exactly why Alessandro had bought it.

Finished with the files, he glanced at Mia, who was

sitting perfectly straight in her seat, legs to the side, ankles neatly crossed, her expression deliberately serene. She looked like a duchess. It annoyed Alessandro, as everything about her seemed to, which was a reaction he knew didn't make sense, and yet it *was*. It was, because he'd much rather be annoyed by her than affected. Which he also was. Unfortunately.

'Thank you for this,' he finally said, his voice clipped.

'Will there be anything else?'

'How well do you know Dillard's clients?'

Surprise rippled across the placid expression on her face, like wind on water, and then she gave a tiny shrug. 'Fairly well, I suppose.'

'Do you interact with them often?'

'When they visit the office, yes. I chat with them, give them coffee, that sort of thing.' She paused, her gaze scanning his face, looking for clues as to what he wanted from her. 'I've also organised the annual summer party for clients and their families, held at Mr Dillard's estate in Surrey, every year.'

'You have?' He would have expected Dillard to hire an event planner for such a high-profile event, but perhaps he was too indifferent even for that. 'That must have been quite time consuming.'

'Yes, but rewarding. I enjoy meeting and seeing the families. I've become friends with some of them, in a professional capacity only, of course. But after seven years, I believe I can say that I know many of them quite well.'

Alessandro could picture it—Mia circulating quietly through the crowds, always at the ready to help, providing whatever was needed—a tissue, a glass of champagne, a shoulder to cry on. Learning the secrets and weaknesses of Dillard's clients and their families, as well as their strengths.

Which made Mia James invaluable…for now. She could help him to get to know Dillard's clients, so he could make a more informed decision about which to pursue or keep.

'So,' Mia asked as he continued to stare at her, his mind clicking over, 'was there anything else you needed?'

'Yes,' Alessandro stated as realisation unfurled and then crystallised inside him. 'Your attendance at a charity gala with me tonight.'

CHAPTER TWO

MIA STARED AT Alessandro's determined, unyielding expression, registering the iron in his eyes, the laser-like
focus of his gaze, and tried to make sense of his request.

'Pardon?' she finally said, wishing she didn't feel
wrong-footed by his invitation. She'd been doing
her best to be the perfect, unflappable PA since he'd
stormed into the office, practically vibrating with energy. At moments like this it felt like no more than a
flimsy façade.

'A charity gala at the Ritz,' Alessandro clarified, his
voice now very slightly edged with impatience, as if she
wasn't catching on quickly enough. 'Many of Dillard's
clients will be there. I'm attending to reassure them of
their assets' safety. You will attend with me.'

A command, then, and one she couldn't afford to dis-
obey. Still, Mia's mind whirled. She'd never attended
such a highbrow function, and in what capacity? As
his PA? *As his date?*

No, of course not. She was mad to think that way
even for a second, and yet somehow the way he'd said
'with me' had felt...

Possessive. As if he were staking his claim on her, branding her with his words.

But of course that wasn't what he meant. The prospect horrified her, and would undoubtedly horrify him even more. Alessandro Costa most certainly didn't think of her like *that*. And she most certainly didn't want him to.

But why did he need her at such an event? When she'd been Henry Dillard's PA, she'd always had a quiet, unnoticeable presence. Invisible on purpose, gliding through the shadows. She'd attended the summer party, yes, but only as the organiser, slipping quietly behind the scenes, doing her best to be both indispensable and out of the way.

She'd never gone to any other of Henry's many social functions—the balls and cocktail parties, fundraisers and expensive, boozy dinners in Michelin-starred restaurants. Of course she hadn't.

'I'm not sure…' she began, and then stopped, because she wasn't sure what she was trying to say. That she wasn't the kind of person he should ask? That she didn't normally go to these events? That she'd be out of her depth? All three, but the last thing she wanted to do was admit her weakness or unsuitability. Alessandro Costa seemed as if he was simply waiting for her to give him one good reason to fire her, and she was determined not to humour him in that regard.

'You're not sure…?' he prompted, an edge to his voice, as if he was daring her.

Mia lifted her chin. 'When is the gala?'

The tiniest smile quirked the corner of his mouth,

electrifying her. The man was devastating already, but heaven help her if he *smiled*. His eyes turned to silver and Mia's insides turned molten. She swallowed audibly and kept her chin up.

'Seven o'clock.'

Mia's mind raced. It was undoubtedly a black-tie event, formal wear absolutely necessary, and her only appropriate outfit was a basic and rather boring black cocktail dress, back at her flat in Wimbledon. It would take nearly an hour to get there, and then back again…

'What is it?' Alessandro demanded, now definitely starting to sound annoyed. 'Why are you looking like this won't be possible, when I can assure you it is?'

'No reason,' Mia said quickly. She'd manage. Somehow she'd manage. 'I'll be ready at seven.'

'Six forty-five,' Alessandro returned. 'On the dot. I like to be punctual.'

Back at her desk Mia couldn't concentrate on anything, not that there was very much for her to do. Like everyone else she was in limbo, waiting to find out how Alessandro Costa decided to handle his new acquisition, and whether they would have jobs come morning.

A few minutes after she'd left the office, Alessandro strode out of it, without sparing her a single glance. As he stepped into the lift, she tried not to notice how the expensive material of his suit stretched across his shoulders, or his dark hair gleamed blue-black in the light. She certainly wasn't going to remember that twang of energy that she'd felt reverberate between them when she'd been standing close enough to inhale the heady scent of his aftershave. No, definitely not noticing any of those things. In fact, she decided, now was as good a time as any to go back to her flat and fetch her dress.

Her heart tumbled in her chest as she grabbed her handbag and headed out, half afraid of running into Alessandro and having to bear the brunt of his ire. It was lunchtime, so she had a reason to be leaving the office, but she still felt nervous about crossing or irritating him in any way. Her job, she acknowledged grimly, was in a very precarious place, no matter how *useful* she seemed to him at the moment.

An hour and a half later, Mia was breathlessly hurrying back into the office, her dress and shoes clutched in a bag to her chest. As the lift doors slid open, she stepped inside—and smack into Alessandro Costa.

The breath left her chest with a startling whoosh, and she would have stumbled had Alessandro not clamped his hands on her shoulders to steady her. For a heart-stopping second his nearness overwhelmed her, the heat and power rolling off him in intoxicating waves. Her mind blurred and then blanked, her palms flat on his very well-muscled chest, fingers stretching instinctively as if to feel more of him. She could not think of a single thing to say. She couldn't even move, conscious only of his powerful, hard body so very near to hers. If she so much as swayed their hips would actually *brush*…

Then Alessandro released her, stepping back, his mouth compressed in a hard line as he raked her with a single, scathing glance. 'Where have you been?'

'I'm sorry, were you looking for me?'

'I wanted the files on Dillard's less impressive clients. Did you think I'd be satisfied with only the top ten?' Even for him, he sounded on edge, his body taut with barely suppressed tension.

'I'm sorry, I was at lunch.'

'For an hour and a half?'

Mia shook her head, a flush fighting its way up her throat and across her face. She'd been afraid of this exact scenario, and now that it was a reality she couldn't handle it. He was still standing so close, and every time she took a breath she inhaled the aroma of his aftershave, felt his heat. 'No, of course not.' She drew herself up, holding onto the last threads of her composure. She could do this. She needed to do this. 'If you must know, I went back to my flat to find a dress to wear this evening. But I will have the other files to you shortly, I promise.'

Alessandro stared at her for another agonising moment before he gave a brief, terse nod. 'Very well. I expect files on all the other clients within the hour. Exactly.'

Mia had no doubt he'd been timing her to the second. The man was a stickler for detail…among other things. Back at her desk she hung her dress up on the back of a door and hurried to amass the files Alessandro had demanded. She'd be hard-pressed to do it in an hour, but she was determined to show Alessandro she could.

Fingers flying, mind racing, she managed to assemble everything and jot down relevant notes, stepping into Henry's—now Alessandro's—office with one minute to spare. Alessandro glanced at his watch as she stepped through the doors, and then one of his faint smiles quirked his mouth for no more than a second, making her catch her breath.

Heaven help her.

'Impressive,' he said after a moment, sounding both amused and reluctantly admiring. 'I didn't think you could do it in an hour.'

'You underestimate me, Mr Costa.'

His gaze lingered on her, and Mia felt her body start to tingle and hum. 'Maybe I do,' he murmured, and held out his hand for the files.

Mia handed them to him, and then took him through each one, making sure to sit on the other side of the desk as he'd requested before.

It was surely better for her to have a little distance between them; being near him had the troubling side-effect of short-circuiting her brain. She didn't know whether it was his intimidating presence, his unde-niable charisma, or the unavoidable fact of his out-rageously good looks that turned her mind to slush, but something about him did, and that was definitely not a good reaction to have to her boss, or even to anyone. Mia never wanted another person to have any power over her—not physical, not emotional, and cer-tainly not sensual. Just thinking about it made goose-pimples rise on her flesh. Alessandro certainly had the last one…if she let him.

'Is there anything else you need?' she asked once they'd gone through all the files, her body tense from holding herself apart and doing her utmost not to notice the powerful muscles of his forearms when he'd rolled up his shirtsleeves, or the stubble now glinting on the hard line of his jaw. No, she was definitely not noticing anything like that.

'Yes,' Alessandro told her shortly. 'Show me your dress.'

Her mouth dropped open before she snapped it shut. 'My…dress?'

'Yes, your dress. I want to make sure it is suitable. As my companion, how you look is important.'

'Your companion…' Her mind spun emptily again. *Surely he wasn't suggesting…?*

'We are attending together,' Alessandro clarified pointedly, as if to highlight the utter impossibility of whatever she might have been thinking. 'You must be suitably attired. Now show me the dress.'

Wordlessly Mia rose from her seat. She had no idea what Alessandro Costa considered *suitably attired*, but she had a feeling her plain black cocktail dress, bought from the bargain rack, wasn't going to be it. Unless he wanted her to be discreet, even invisible, as Henry Dillard had? As she was used to being from childhood, slipping in and out of the shadows, trying not to draw attention to herself, in case she provoked her father's anger? Because in all truth she wasn't sure she knew how to be anything else.

She grabbed the dress and returned to the office, holding it in front of her. 'Will this do?' she asked, unable to keep the faintest tremble from her voice. She'd never had her boss vet her clothing choices before, and she didn't like it. She certainly didn't like feeling controlled, even in as small a matter as this. She'd had enough of that in her life, and she didn't want or need any more, not even by the boss whose good side she was trying to stay on.

'You intended to wear *that*?' Alessandro sounded both scandalised and completely derisive. 'Did you want to be mistaken for one of the serving staff?'

Mia's chin went up. 'It's perfectly appropriate.'

'It's perfectly dreadful, like something a junior secretary would wear to the office Christmas party.'

She *had* worn it to such a party, and so Mia did not deign to reply to his remark. Alessandro might be offensively blunt, but there was more perception and truth to his remarks than she wanted to acknowledge.

'You can't wear it,' he stated. 'You won't.'

'I don't have anything else,' Mia returned. 'So if you wish for me to attend…'

'Then I will make sure you do have something.' He slid his phone out of his pocket. 'I will not have you on my arm looking like Cinderella still in her rags.'

'So you'll be my fairy godmother?' Mia quipped before she could attempt a more measured reply. What was it about this man that made her hackles rise, everything in her resist? Henry Dillard had certainly never made her respond like this, but then Henry Dillard had never spoken to her in such an arrogant, autocratic way. He'd been affably incompetent, content to let her organise everything.

Alessandro's eyes gleamed like molten silver as his mouth quirked the tiniest bit, making her respond to him. *Again*. A very inconvenient response, when her stomach fizzed and her heart leapt. Mia was determined to ignore it. 'Now, that is the first time anyone has called me that,' he said, his mouth curving deeper, and Mia forced herself to look away.

Alessandro angled his body away from Mia as he spoke into the phone, asking for a personal stylist to be brought to the office immediately. His right-hand man, Luca, took the rather unexpected request in his stride.

Ending the call, Alessandro turned back to face Mia, trying not to notice the rise and fall of her chest with every agitated breath she took; clearly she didn't like him deciding what she should wear, although she should be thankful he'd vetted her selection. That black bag of a dress looked cheap and boring and was hardly what he needed his companion for the evening to turn up in.

'As your PA, I don't see why I need to wear some fancy dress,' Mia said, clearly striving to moderate her tone. 'Or, in fact, why I need to attend this gala at all. It's highly unusual…'

'You need to attend because many of the guests there will be Dillard's clients,' Alessandro answered. 'And you will know them better than I do. I require your knowledge in this matter.'

'Still…'

'And you need to wear a gown worthy of the occasion,' Alessandro cut across her. He didn't like her protestations; he was used to being obeyed instantly, and Mia James seemed not to have realised that.

'The clients will know I'm Henry's PA,' she protested. 'If I dress up like a proper guest, they'll think I'm putting on airs—'

'You are my PA now, and you are my guest,' Alessandro returned. 'You will wear an appropriate gown. I am sure there will be something you fancy from the selection provided.' He gave her a quelling look. 'Most women I know would be thrilled to have such an opportunity of choice.'

'Somehow I don't think I'm like most women you know,' Mia returned tartly, making him smile.

'That is very true. Even so, I would like you to pick a dress that is suitable.'

Mia nodded, setting her jaw, her eyes sparking like bits of blue ice. 'Very well,' she said, sounding far from pleased about the matter. Despite the difficulties of the situation, Alessandro would have thought she'd enjoy the opportunity to select a new gown.

'The stylist will be here shortly,' he told her. 'Until then you may return to your work.'

With a brief, brisk nod Mia swivelled on her heel and walked out of the office, closing the door behind her with a firm click that was halfway to becoming a slam. It annoyed and amused Alessandro in equal measure. Normally he didn't like people to oppose him; in fact, he hated any sign of disobedience or disrespect.

As he was a man of both drive and focus, work was a well-oiled machine and rebelliousness was inefficient as well as time-consuming. And, while Mia's rebelliousness did annoy him, that contrary spark of defiance somehow...*enflamed* him.

The knowledge rested uncomfortably with him. He

was attracted to her, he acknowledged starkly, and that was something he most certainly could and would control. There was no place for attraction within the workplace, and self-control had always been his personal creed, the way he lived his life. The way he stayed on top.

He would never, ever be like his mother, whose sorry life had been tossed on the waves of other people's whims, her poverty and powerlessness making her constantly vulnerable, searching for love and meaning in shabby, shallow relationships.

Alessandro would never be like that…never at another person's mercy…not even for the sake of a very inconvenient desire.

Still, he was uncomfortably aware of the simple *fact* of his attraction, as well as the realisation that his desire to see Mia attired in an appropriate gown was not quite as professional and expedient as he'd made it seem.

As she'd pointed out herself, she was known as Dillard's PA and a simple, serviceable dress would certainly have been adequate. Yet he hadn't wanted to see his date in something resembling a bin bag. He hadn't wanted to see *Mia* in it.

Still, he told himself, he needed to make the right impression tonight. The last thing he wanted was for people to look at him and think that an impostor had shown up along with his secretary. Because Alessandro had earned the right to be at the party, just as he'd earned the right to be sitting in the office. Just as he'd earned everything he had, fighting for it and winning it, time and time again, a man with a mission. A man who won.

A few minutes later Luca texted him that the stylist had arrived, and Alessandro rose to find Mia. She was at her desk, and as he came to stand behind her, glancing at the screen of her laptop, a cold wave of displeasure and shock rippled through him.

'You're working on your CV?'

She swivelled sharply in her chair, her eyes widening with alarm at the sight of him looking at the screen, but when she spoke her voice was cool. 'For when I'm no longer *useful*.'

'And that is not now.' With one brisk movement Alessandro clicked the mouse to close the document, without saving any changes. Mia's mouth compressed but she did not protest against his action. 'The stylist is here. You may use my office.'

Mia's eyes flashed and he wondered what she objected to—his dismissal of her dress, or his order for a new one? Or simply his manner, which was even more autocratic than usual, because it felt like the best defence against this irritating and inconvenient attraction that simmered beneath the surface, threatening to bubble up?

Even now he found himself sneaking looks at the tantalising vee of ivory skin visible at the all too modest neck of her blouse, and noting the soft curve of her jaw, and the way a wisp of golden hair had fallen against her cheek. He itched to tuck it behind her ear, let his fingers skim to her lobe, a prospect which was too bizarre to be entertained even for a second.

He didn't want to do things like that. *Ever.* Relationships were not on his radar, and sex was nothing more than a physical urge to be sated like any other. He'd always been able to find women who were agreeable to his terms. More than agreeable, so why was he feeling this strange way about Mia James?

He wasn't. Or at least he wouldn't. He wouldn't let himself. Work was too important to risk for a moment's satisfaction, even with someone as annoyingly beguiling as the woman in front of him.

'Are you coming?' he asked tersely, and she nodded, rising from her seat with unconscious elegance, following him with a graceful, long-legged stride. Alessandro found himself watching the gentle sway of her hips before he resolutely turned his gaze away.

A few minutes later the stylist arrived with a flurry of plastic-swathed hangers, an assistant behind her carrying several boxes and bags. Alessandro supervised their setting up before he decided to leave Mia to it.

'Let me see your final choice,' he instructed, and she arched one golden eyebrow.

'To approve it?'

'Of course.' That was the point of this whole exercise, was it not? Still, he decided to temper his reply, for her benefit. 'Thank you for attending to this matter.'

She pressed her lips together. 'It's not as if I had much choice.'

Alessandro frowned. 'I'm offering you a *dress.* Is that so objectionable?'

'It's not the dress and you know it,' she snapped, and surprisingly, he let out a laugh.

'No, I suppose not.'

'It's your entire manner,' she emphasised, and he nodded.

'Yes, I realise,' he said dryly. 'So at least we're in agreement about something.'

For the next few hours he found he could not concentrate on the business at hand, a fact which annoyed him as much as everything else about Mia James had done. What was it about the woman that got under his skin, burrowed deep inside? Was it simply her attractiveness, which was undeniable, or something else? The hint of defiance in the set of her shoulders, the surprising vulnerability he sensed beneath the surface? Why on earth did he *care*?

It was annoying. It was alarming. And it had to stop.

'Mr Costa?' The stylist's fluttering voice interrupted his unruly thoughts; he'd been staring at his laptop screen for who knew how long? 'Miss James has selected her dress and is ready for you to see it.'

'Thank you.' He rose and walked quickly to the office, steeling himself for whatever he was to see. Despite his best intention to remain utterly unmoved, he was still shocked by the sight of her, her slender body swathed in an ice-blue gown of ruched silk that hugged her figure before flaring out around her ankles in a decadent display of iridescent, shimmering material. Instead of back in a sedate clip, her hair was twisted into an elegant chignon. Diamonds sparkled at her ears and throat. She looked like a Norse goddess, an ice queen, everything about her coolly beautiful, icily intoxicating.

Desire crashed over him in an overwhelming wave,

unexpected even now in its intensity and force. He wanted to pluck the diamond-tipped pins from her hair. He wanted to tug on the discreet zip in the back of her dress, and count the sharp knobs of her vertebrae, taste the smooth silkiness of her skin.

He *wanted*. And he never let himself want.

'Well?' Mia asked, her voice taut. 'Will I pass?'

'Yes,' he answered after another beat of tense silence, barely managing to get the word out. 'You'll pass.'

She let out a huff of sound, turning away from him, and the stylist's face fell a little bit at his damningly faint praise. Alessandro didn't care. Already he was regretting his command to have Mia accompany him tonight. Already he was looking forward to it far more than he should.

'I'll go and change myself,' he said when a few seconds had ticked by without anyone saying a word. 'Be ready to leave in ten minutes.'

Mia nodded, not quite looking at him, and again Alessandro was captivated by the curve of her jaw, the hollow of her throat, the dip of her waist, each one begging to be explored and savoured. He turned away quickly, striding out of the office without another word.

The sooner this evening was over, the better. This desire he felt was inconvenient and overwhelming and very much unwanted. But, like everything else in his life, he would control it. It would just take a little more effort than he'd anticipated.

CHAPTER THREE

MIA FELT AS if she'd fallen down a rabbit hole into some strange, charmed alternative reality...a reality where she rode in limousines, and drank champagne, and walked into a glittering ballroom on the arm of the most handsome man there.

Of course, as PA to Henry Dillard she'd ridden in plenty of limousines. She'd drunk more than enough champagne. But it had always been as an employee, someone to serve and be invisible while she was at it. Someone to make sure the champagne was flowing, and that the limousine arrived on time. Someone who didn't stride into parties, but sidled along the sidelines, checking that everything was going according to plan and keeping out of the way.

Tonight was entirely different. Tonight, much to her own amazement, she felt like the belle of the ball. It was beyond bizarre. It was also intoxicating, far more than any champagne she might quaff.

It had started with the stylist bringing out several exquisite dresses for Mia to choose from, and then doing her hair and make-up as well, before finishing off her incredible ensemble with the most beautiful diamond earrings and necklace Mia had ever seen.

As someone who had prided herself on always being smart and sensible, no-nonsense and pragmatic, it had felt to her as decadent as an endless dark chocolate sundae to be so pampered and primped. She hadn't expected to enjoy it; she'd been fully intent on chafing at every opportunity, resenting Alessandro's needless autocratic intervention, but then…she hadn't.

She'd submitted to the stylist's every instruction, and then she'd started to enjoy it. To *relish* it. Part of her was horrified by her own acquiescence, and what it might mean. And yet…it was one night. One magical night after a lifetime of having her head down, working hard. Why shouldn't she enjoy it?

At some point she'd let her mind slide into a comforting sort of blurry nothingness, floating on a sea of ease and comfort. As she usually tried to anticipate every possibility, consider every choice, it felt wonderfully relaxing not to overthink this. She wasn't going to wonder what Alessandro Costa wanted with her, or with Dillard Investments, or whether her job, not to mention any of her friends', was secure. She was just going to enjoy a night like no other, because she doubted she'd see another one like it, and that was fine.

And then the moment when Alessandro had come into the room and looked her over…that moment had felt as if the world was tilting on its axis, as if everything was sliding away from the comforting security of its anchor even as it came into glittering focus.

For that one second Mia had seen a flash of masculine approval blaze in his eyes like golden fire and it had ignited her right through, as her blood heated and fizzed and her mind spun out possibilities she'd never dared to dream of.

Then he'd told her she'd pass, his voice as laconic as ever, and she'd wondered if she'd imagined it. She must have. This was *Alessandro Costa*, after all. The ruthless, arrogant CEO she was a little bit scared of. Not a man interested in her. Not her *date*.

It just felt as if he were. And, more alarmingly, she *liked* that feeling. She, who had steered clear of love and romance and even anything close to a flirtation, because she did not want someone to have that kind of power over her. Because her mother had fallen in love with her father all those years ago, and look how that had gone.

'He loves me, Mia. Really. He just has trouble showing it.'

Mia had listened to far too many of her mother's excuses before she'd died of cancer when Mia was fourteen, too broken and despairing to hold on any longer. Mia had had to wait four more years before she was finally free of her father's sneering control. And since then she'd made it her life's mission to stay strong, independent and alone. *Safe.*

But tonight she let her rules bend and even break. Tonight she let herself forget they existed. It was just a night, after all. Just one wonderful night where she could pretend, for a few hours, that she was a young woman with a gorgeous man, Cinderella with her prince before the clock inevitably struck midnight.

They'd ridden in a limousine to the Ritz, and Alessandro, devastating in black tie, his hair midnight-dark and his hard jaw freshly shaven, had barely said a word, which was fine by Mia because she could barely think. Dressed to the nines and even the tens in a gorgeous gown, on the arm of a beautiful man…going to the kind of party where she'd normally be holding doors or serving champagne…together, all of it, was utterly overwhelming. Intoxicating. *Wonderful.*

A valet had opened the door of the limousine as they'd pulled up to the front entrance of the hotel, and flashbulbs had popped and sparked as Mia had stepped out, blinking in the glare. She wasn't used to the spotlight; she always stood to one side, watched it from afar. It felt very different to be the one basking in the bright light, especially when Alessandro had slid his arm through hers and smiled for the cameras, their heads nearly touching.

What was he doing? And why?

She still didn't really understand the need for her presence at the ball. Yes, she knew Dillard's clients, but she'd already given Alessandro all the relevant information in the files. And this was a charity event, not a business meeting. Surely he had someone else, a dozen 'someone elses', to accompany him to such a glittering occasion, a supermodel or socialite who would fit in more easily with all this well-heeled crowd? Mia didn't know how to rub shoulders with these people; she was used to fetching them coffee. She was out of her depth, and she never felt it more so than when Alessandro approached a group of people, some of whom she knew, and introduced her as his 'companion'.

Mia clocked the raised eyebrows, the curious smiles, the speculative looks, and like everyone else in the group she wondered what Alessandro Costa was playing at.

'Why don't you just tell people I'm your PA?' she asked when they had a moment alone. She'd drunk two glasses of champagne in quick succession, more to have something to do than because of any desire to be drunk, but now her head was spinning, her tongue loosened.

'Because tonight you are a beautiful woman who is accompanying me to a gala.'

'But...' She shook her head slowly, trying to discern the emotion behind his cool, mask-like exterior, his eyes like blank mirrors. The man gave absolutely nothing away. 'Why?'

He shrugged his powerful shoulders, muscles rippling under the expensive material of his tuxedo. 'Why not?'

'You seem like a man who has a very clear reason for everything he does,' Mia said slowly. 'So your "why not?" doesn't actually hold water with me.'

'Oh?' One dark slash of an eyebrow arched in cool amusement. 'You surprise me with your perception, Miss James.'

'If I'm your companion, perhaps you should call me Mia.'

Something flickered in his eyes, and Mia felt a shiver through her belly in response. She hadn't meant to sound flirtatious, but she realised she might have... and she didn't actually mind. 'Very well,' Alessandro said after a moment. 'Mia.' His voice, with his slight accent, seemed to caress the two syllables.

'Where are you from?' Mia asked. 'It didn't say when I looked online.'

His eyebrow arched higher. 'You did a search on me?'

She shrugged. 'After I heard you'd taken over the company, yes, of course. Information is power.'

'True.' His gaze held hers, his expression considering. 'And is that what you want? Power?'

'I want to keep my job,' Mia said after a second's pause. 'And knowing my employer helps with that.'

'Mia!' A woman approached them in a flurry of cloying scent, kissing Mia on both cheeks while Alessandro stepped back discreetly. 'Darling, how are you? I heard about poor Henry…'

Mia shot an alarmed look at Alessandro; his expression seemed dangerously neutral. 'Diane,' she said, after she'd returned the woman's tight hug. 'This is Alessandro Costa, the new CEO of Dillard Investments.'

'New…*oh*.' Diane Holley's mouth dropped into a comical 'o' as she swivelled to face Alessandro, her eyes widening in shocked speculation.

'Pleased to meet you…?'

'Diane. Diane Holley.' She took Alessandro's outstretched hand, looking a bit dazed. As Diane shook his hand, Mia saw her expression change from surprise to admiration, her lowered gaze sweeping speculatively, and almost avariciously, over Alessandro Costa's admittedly impressive form. 'Very pleased to meet you too, of course…' she murmured.

Mia felt a sharp tug of jealousy, a reaction which surprised and appalled her in equal measure. *What on earth...?* She had absolutely no reason to feel remotely jealous in any way. She didn't *care* about Alessandro Costa. She didn't even like the man. And jealousy was not an emotion she'd ever let herself entertain. It was so weak and needy. It was also dangerous.

And yet...she was wearing a beautiful dress, and he'd looked at her, for a brief second, with desire in his eyes, and for a single evening she'd felt like someone else entirely, someone transported into a fairy tale, from the shadows to the spotlight.

Perhaps one evening was too much, after all. The last thing she needed to do was lose her head, even for an evening, over Alessandro Costa. The man was too dangerous, and too much was at risk. Not just her job, but her very self. She couldn't let Alessandro Costa affect her. Make her want. Make her weak. Not even for a moment.

Then he put another flute of champagne into her hand, and her fingers closed around the fragile crystal stem automatically. 'You looked as if you were a million miles away,' he murmured, his voice low and honeyed. 'Don't you like hearing about Diane Holley's corgis?'

'Corgis?' Blinking, Mia realised Diane must have been chatting to Alessandro for a few minutes at least and she hadn't taken in a word. The older woman, the wife of one of Dillard's most important clients, had already moved on. 'She told you about her corgis?'

'I asked about them. You mentioned them this afternoon.'

'Did I?'

Alessandro arched an eyebrow, looking more amused than annoyed—for once. 'You really haven't been paying attention, have you?'

'Of course I have. I always do.' She took a defiant sip of champagne. 'Diane has four corgis, and one of them has digestive issues.'

'She didn't mention those tonight, thankfully.'

'You were lucky, then.' Mia's breath came out in a surprised hiss as Alessandro took her elbow, his hand warm and dry and so very sure as he steered her towards another cluster of people. 'Where…where are we going?'

'To mingle, of course. That's why we're here. You're going to introduce me to all these people, and then tell me their secrets.'

'I thought I'd already done that this afternoon. Besides, I don't know any secrets.'

'I still need to put names to faces. And I think you know more secrets than you realise…always working behind the scenes, listening in the shadows.'

'You make me sound like a snoop.'

'No, someone who is smart.' His gaze lingered on hers for a tantalising second as his hand had moved from her elbow to her waist, his fingers splayed across her hip. Heat flooded Mia's body, and once again she was in danger of drifting along this lovely tide of feeling. 'Mr Costa…'

'You must call me Alessandro.'

'*You* must stop acting like I'm your date.' She knew she never would have said the words if she hadn't had two glasses of champagne, and just chugged half of her third. If she wasn't so afraid of how much he affected her.

'Why? You are my date.' He sounded utterly unruffled, like someone making a simple statement of fact.

'No…' Her breath came out in a rush. Her head spun. People were *looking* at them. Wondering. 'I'm not. Not really…'

'Yes, you are.' They'd reached the group of people, and Alessandro kept his hand on her waist as he stretched out his other one. 'Alessandro Costa, CEO of Dillard Investments.' In turn, everyone shook his hand, with varying expressions of pleasure, speculation, or snobbery. It made Mia wonder yet again about Alessandro. What was he doing here, exactly? Why did he want her with him? Who *was* this man at her side? And how much did she want to know?

The chit-chat washed over her as she took in Alessandro's easy, urbane manner. The man could be charming when he chose, a fact that alarmed her. If Alessandro Costa affected her when he was blunt and brusque, heaven help her when he was easy and affable.

She knew a few people in the group through Dillard's, and somehow, her mind still spinning, she made chit-chat, introduced Alessandro to a few others, and stumbled through the evening, feeling as if she were acting a part in a play, desperate now to get to the end of the evening without embarrassing herself or losing her head entirely over the man at her side.

When they were alone again, and she was finishing her third glass of champagne, she rather recklessly asked him about it all.

'I can make conversation, if that's what you mean,' he answered as he sipped his own champagne.

'What do you want from these people?' Mia asked, her tongue well and truly loosened by now. 'Why did you buy Dillard Investments, really?'

A guarded look came over his face before he shrugged, the movement clearly meant to be dismissive. 'Why do I buy any company?'

'You tell me.'

The tiniest of pauses. 'For financial gain.'

'But you said yourself Dillard's was operating at a loss.'

'That doesn't mean it always has to.'

'Still…' She shook her head slowly. 'A man like you…'

'A man like me?' Alessandro's voice sharpened. 'What does that mean, exactly?'

'Only that you must always have your eye on the bottom line.'

'True.' He eyed her thoughtfully. 'So what did you learn about me, during that online cyberstalking session?'

Mia let out a choked laugh. 'I was hardly *stalking*.'

'Weren't you?'

'Gathering information. Big difference.'

'Hmm.' She felt dizzy with the turn in their conversation. It almost felt as if…as if they were flirting. But of course they couldn't be. 'So,' Alessandro asked, stepping closer, 'what did you learn about me, Mia?'

* * *

Alessandro hadn't meant to ask the question. He surely didn't mean to bother with the answer. He was curious despite his determination never to be curious about anyone. Curiosity implied caring, and he didn't care. And yet… 'Anything interesting?' The words sounded provocative.

Mia licked her lips, her tongue looking very pink as she touched it to her full, lush lips, the instinctive movement causing a dart of desire to arrow through him, unsettling in its intensity. 'Not really.' Her gaze skittered away from his. 'Not much.'

'Tell me.' His voice was low, the words a command, but with a thread of something dark and rich running through it, a promise he hadn't meant to make. Mia turned to look at him, her eyes widening, looking very blue and clear. Eyes he could drown in if he let himself. He stepped closer. 'Tell me,' he said again.

'Well…' Again her tongue touched her lips. 'You have a reputation for being ruthless. You take over companies, strip them of their assets, and fire about ninety percent of the staff before absorbing the company into Costa International.'

That was the gist without being entirely true, but Alessandro wasn't about to defend his actions. They spoke for themselves.

'Are you going to do that with Dillard's?' Her chin lifted a little. 'Fire everyone? Get rid of it all?'

He eyed her for a moment, considering what to tell her. For some contrary reason he didn't like the thought of her thinking badly of him, which was ridiculous, because he'd been thought of far worse by the furious CEOs he'd displaced.

'I'm not going to fire everyone,' he said at last. 'I never do.'

'Ninety percent, then.'

'Your percentages are a bit off.'

'Do you enjoy it?' she asked, her voice choking. 'Ruining people's lives?'

He stared at her for a moment, fighting the urge to explain the truth of his mission. But, no. He was not going to justify himself to her. He was certainly not going to care about her opinion. 'Does it seem as if I do?' he asked, meaning to sound dismissive.

Slowly she shook her head. 'You don't actually seem *cruel*.'

'No?' He tried to keep his voice disinterested.

'The media portrayed you as a bit of a cowboy… someone who came from nowhere and had a meteoric rise. Not entirely respectable, but not cruel.'

'Well, they were wrong,' Alessandro said lightly, even though her words were like razors on his skin. 'I'm not at all respectable.'

'Is that why you took Dillard's over? To seem respectable?'

The question grated. As if he wanted to don Dillard's shabby suit and call himself a gentleman. 'Not at all. I don't care one iota if I seem respectable or not.'

'Then why bother with them? Where is the profit?'

'In the clients I keep.' Although Alessandro suspected there would be little profit indeed. Profit was not why he did what he did, at least not in regard to companies such as Dillard's.

'And what about all the employees? Innocent people...don't you care about them?'

More than she would ever know. 'You're sounding like a crusader, Mia,' he warned her. He did not wish to discuss this any longer. 'It's quite dull.'

Her eyes flashed. 'So sorry I'm boring you, but people's lives are at stake. Besides... I would have thought you might understand how they felt.'

He tensed, the perception in her eyes like a needle burrowing into his skin. 'Oh?'

'The media said you came from a poor background... the slums of Naples.' He angled his head away from her, not trusting the expression on his face. 'Is that true?'

'Slums is such a pejorative word, but I suppose, in essence, yes.' He did his best to sound bored. He *was* bored.

The last thing he wanted to talk about was his pathetic past...the endless chaos of moving from grotty flat to grotty flat, the stints in foster care when his mother had lost custody of him, the endless jobs she'd taken cleaning office buildings, the countless boyfriends she'd had in a desperate bid to assuage the despairing sadness of her life. A childhood he'd done his best always to remember, to remind him of how he would be different, even as he pretended to forget.

'Then if you know what it's like to be poor, to live from pay check to pay check, how can you fire people like that?'

'Because I know what it's like to work hard,' he said

in a steely voice, 'and to earn what I have. And anyone who does those things will have a position with Costa International, that much I guarantee.'

Her eyes widened. 'They will?'

She sounded so hopeful it made him cringe. 'Dillard Investments was dying on the vine. I just plucked it before it fell, withered, to the ground. If anything, I've *saved* people's jobs in the long run.'

'Do you really mean that?'

Impatient now, he shrugged. 'Henry Dillard was charming, I'll grant you that, but he was a terrible businessman. I did his employees a favour.' *Why* had he stooped to justifying himself? 'I'm not the monster you seem to think I am,' he finished levelly. 'Regardless of what you read online.'

She stared at him for a moment, and he felt as if she were seeing right inside him, that blue, blue gaze burrowing deep down inside his soul, reaching places he'd closed off for good. He looked away, shrugging as he took a sip of champagne, struggling to master his wayward emotions.

'No,' she said softly. 'I don't think you are.'

'You've changed your mind?' He'd meant to sound offhand and failed.

'I think you like to present yourself as someone hardened and ruthless,' she said slowly. 'It's the right image for someone who specialises in corporate takeovers, isn't it?'

'I suppose.' What else could he say? She saw too much already.

'I wonder who you really are,' she murmured. 'I won-

der what you're hiding.' Alessandro stared at her, unable
to look away. He felt a tug low in his belly, pulling him
towards her. She wanted to *know* him. It was beguiling,
alarming. Nobody knew him, not like that.

'Let's dance,' he said, his voice roughened with
emotion. When they danced, they wouldn't talk. She
wouldn't say things or see inside him. He would make
sure of it.

Wordlessly Mia nodded, and after depositing their
empty champagne flutes on a nearby table, Alessandro
took her by the hand and led her to the ballroom's par-
quet dance floor. The music was a slow, sensuous piece,
the sonorous wail of a saxophone wrapping its lonely
notes around them as Alessandro took her into his arms.

Her hips bumped his gently and heat flared white-
hot, making his hands tense on hers before he deliberately relaxed his grip and began to move her around
the floor.

She was elegant in his arms, matching the rhythm of
his movements, her hips swaying, her body lithe. Lithe
and eager. He felt her tremble and knew, like him, she
felt this most inconvenient and heady desire, growing
stronger with every second they swayed together. The
realisation only stoked his own.

Sex, for him, had always been a matter of expedi-
ency, a physical need to be met like any other—food,
water, sleep, sex. That was how he'd viewed it. Something to be ticked off, the same as he would with a physical workout or a medical examination.

This felt different. *More.* This desire, twining
through him like some dangerous vine, felt capable of

overwhelming him. Overtaking the rational thought, common sense and, far worse, the self-control that were the touchstones of his life, the anchors of his soul. And the most alarming part was, in this moment he didn't even think he cared.

The pressures of overseeing the takeover, the twenty-hour work days and the ceaseless striving, for years now, decades…in this moment he sloughed it all off like an old skin, let it slither about him in dead, dried peels, as desire birthed him anew.

The song ended and another started, and still they kept dancing. He pulled her closer, so her body nestled into his. She came willingly, twining her arms around his neck, her breasts brushing his chest. Her head was slightly bowed, so he could see the delicate, vulnerable curve of her neck and he had the nearly irresistible urge to press his lips there, against the skin he knew would be warm and soft and silky.

They twirled around again, and she shifted in his arms, the material of her dress rustling and sliding, pulling taut across her breasts, revealing the pure line of her collarbone. He could press his lips there too.

He could do it, and in the haze of his desire, as well as his exhaustion and the champagne he had drunk, he couldn't remember a single reason not to.

The music swelled and the world around him fell away. There was nothing but this. *Her.* They turned again, her dress flaring out from her ankles, brushing his legs.

Some last, desperate part of him tried to claw back his sanity, his sense. This was a bad idea. A terrible,

terrible idea. Mia James worked for him, and he never mixed business with pleasure. Ever. It was far too dangerous. The last thing he needed was a woman at work laying claim to any part of him, or, heaven forbid, accusing him of something.

But there was nothing accusatory in the way Mia was melting into him, her body pliant and willing in his arms. Then she lifted her head, tilting her face upwards, her gaze clashing and then tangling with his.

It felt as if they shared an entire conversation in that silent gaze, a shared yearning and a deeper need, a question and an answer, all encapsulated in a single, burning glance.

Neither of them said a word, but Alessandro felt a shudder run through her as he held her in his arms. The last part of his sanity trickled away. He didn't care.

He didn't care.

'Let's go,' he said, his voice rough with need.

'Where?' Even with her in his arms, he strained to hear her breathy whisper.

'Anywhere.'

Her eyes widened, her lips parting. She swallowed, and he waited for her answer, the one she'd already given in the silent yearning of her gaze. The song ended, and their bodies stilled. Still Alessandro waited, his breath held, his body taut.

Then wordlessly, her eyes wide, Mia nodded.

Alessandro didn't wait for more. Taking her by the hand, he led her from the dance floor and out of the ballroom, out of the hotel, into the warm spring night.

CHAPTER FOUR

THE COOL NIGHT air felt like a slap on her face as Mia left the hotel, Alessandro clasping her hand tightly. It felt like an urgent and much-needed wake-up call.

What on earth was she doing?

What madness had possessed her up there in the ballroom, with the music and the champagne and the slow sway of Alessandro's body in rhythm with hers?

A limousine pulled up to the kerb; Alessandro must have texted his driver while she'd been in this heady daze of desire, a fog that had wrapped her up in its sensuous, blinding warmth, making her immune to everything, including her own common sense. Wordlessly he opened the door and ushered her into the sumptuous leather interior.

Mia slid to the far side of the limo, shivering slightly in the still cool air, despite the sudden blast of warmth from the heater. Now that she was no longer in Alessandro's arms, in that strange, suspended, otherworldly reality…she realised there was no way she could go anywhere or do anything with Alessandro Costa. No matter how she felt. No matter what she'd wanted.

Already she cursed herself for having danced with him at all, swaying in his arms, moving closer, falling under his sensual spell.

What had she been thinking? He was her *boss*, and not a particularly pleasant boss at that, even if she now questioned whether he was as ruthless as he'd been rumoured to be.

Even so, getting involved with him in any capacity would be a serious, serious mistake, and one she had never intended on making with *anyone*. She sneaked a glance at his harsh profile, wondering what he was thinking, now that they were away from the ball, the music and champagne. Was he having second thoughts as she was? Regrets?

'Where…?' Her voice came out scratchy and she licked her lips. 'Where are we going?'

'Back to the office.' Alessandro spoke tersely, and when he turned to her there was something hard and resolute in his face, and his eyes looked dark and flat. Looking at him, taking in that unyielding expression, Mia felt chilled. Clearly he was having second thoughts as well, a thought that should bring sweet, sweet relief, but instead she felt disappointed.

Stupid, stupid.

They rode in silence to the Dillard building in Mayfair, the night a blur of dark sky and city lights all around them. The air in the back of the limo felt taut with tension, and Mia let out a quiet sigh of relief when the limo finally pulled up in front of the office.

'I need to get my things,' she murmured. She'd left her work clothes, coat, and handbag at the office, an oversight she hadn't even considered when she'd been dazzled by being the belle of the ball. The party was well and truly over now, the clock striking midnight, everything turning back to the way it was. There seemed to be no question of their going anywhere together, as Alessandro had hinted at the ball. All Mia wanted to do was go home.

'I need to get my things as well,' Alessandro replied. 'I'll let you go up, and the limo can drive you home.'

'There's no need...' Mia began half-heartedly, feeling she should take the tube as a matter of principle, and after giving her a hard look, Alessandro shrugged, supremely indifferent.

'As you like.'

He swiped his key card and ushered her inside the building, everything now cloaked in darkness and quiet. Mia had been in the office late at night before, when she'd had to work longer hours for one reason or another, but it felt different now, with Alessandro walking right behind her, and gooseflesh rippling over her skin at the knowledge of him being so close.

The lift had never felt so small or suffocating as they rode up in a silence taut not with expectation but the sudden, unsettling lack of it. Then the doors swished open and they stepped onto the top floor of the building, where Henry's office was located. Mia walked through the dim open-plan space, lit only by the streetlights outside, thankful that this ordeal was almost over.

She'd come so close to losing her mind and heaven knew what else over this man. She could consider herself lucky, she told herself, even if she didn't feel all that lucky right then.

'I left my things in Henry's—I mean your—office,' she said, and Alessandro merely nodded as he opened the door and ushered her through. He flicked on a table lamp, bathing the room in warm light, while Mia hurriedly hunted for her bag and discarded clothes. She hesitated, knowing she didn't want to brave the tube home at ten o'clock at night in a floor-length evening gown.

'Do you mind if I change...?'

Another hard, fathomless look, another shrug. 'As you like.' He left the office, and Mia let out another sigh of relief and pent-up tension as the door closed behind him. Her head still felt fuzzy from the champagne, even though the main part of her was stone-cold sober, longing only to be curled up in her bed with a comforting mug of hot chocolate, this whole evening behind her.

Her fingers fumbled as she unclasped the diamond necklace that now felt heavy and cold around her neck. Carefully she replaced it in the black velvet box the stylist had brandished so proudly just a few short hours ago. It felt like another lifetime. Had she really danced with Alessandro? Flirted with him? Felt she had a connection with him, that something important and intimate had pulsed between them when she'd told him she didn't know who he was? And then she'd twined her arms around his neck and told him she'd go anywhere with him. She'd even believed it.

Her breath came out in a shuddery rush as she acknowledged the folly of her actions. She had done all those things and more, and all she could do now was thank heaven that it hadn't gone any further, and that Alessandro at least seemed to have had the same second thoughts she had.

The best-case scenario now was that they would both pretend to forget everything that had—and hadn't—happened. And really, she told herself, it wasn't as if they'd actually *done* anything. They hadn't even kissed.

But she'd wanted to...

Forcing those pointless, treacherous thoughts away, Mia took off the diamond earrings and put them back as well. Then her heels, silver diamanté-decorated stilettos, and her sheer tights, bundling up the tights and putting the shoes back in the box. Now the dress.

She reached behind her to unzip the dress, her fingertips brushing the top of the zipper but unable to pull it down. Mia groaned under her breath, nearly wrenching her arm out of its socket as she tried again, desperately, to unzip her gown. No luck. She couldn't do it on her own. And she couldn't go on the tube in this. She was going to have to ask Alessandro to help her, a prospect that filled her with dread as well as a tiny, treacherous flicker of excitement she chose to ignore.

Alessandro rapped sharply on the door. 'Are you nearly ready?'

'Yes.' Her voice wavered and she took a deep breath before going to the door and opening it. Alessandro stood there, frowning at the sight of her.

'You haven't changed.' He sounded disapproving.

'I know. I can't manage the zip of the dress.' She met his gaze even though it took effort. 'Do you mind helping me?'

'With the zip?'

Why did he sound so surprised, so scandalised? 'Yes,' Mia answered, and then, pointlessly, 'I'm sorry.'

Wordlessly Alessandro nodded and stepped into the room. Mia took another deep breath as she silently turned around, showing him the zip that ran from the nape of her neck to the small of her back.

Moonlight poured through the windows, bathing everything in silver, as for a hushed moment neither of them moved. A tendril of hair had fallen from her chignon and Alessandro moved it from her neck, making her shudder.

She hadn't meant to, heaven knew, she *hadn't*, but the response rippled through her all the same, visceral and consuming, and more importantly audible.

What was it about this man that made her respond this way? She never had before, not even close. Her romantic and sexual experience was basically nil, and that by her choice. Perhaps that was why she was reacting the way she was now, because she had nothing to compare it to.

And yet Mia knew it wasn't that. It was the man. The man whose sandalwood aftershave she breathed in, making her senses reel. The man who was now tugging the zipper down her back, slowly, so achingly slowly, inch by tempting, traitorous, *lovely* inch. *Tug. Tug.* Mia held her breath as Alessandro's breath fanned her neck, and then her bare back as the dress began to fall away, leaving her skin exposed.

The air was cool on her bared back, but Alessandro's breath was warm. Mia tensed, trying to keep herself from shuddering again, but she failed, a ripple of long-ing trembling over her skin and right through her. She knew Alessandro saw and heard it, felt it even.

And she felt his response in the sudden stilling of his fingers on the small of her back, the zip almost all the way undone. Still he didn't move, and Mia didn't either.

The world felt stilled, suspended; everything a hushed, held breath as they both remained where they were, *waiting*. Mia knew she should step away, just as she knew she wouldn't. Couldn't. In fact, she did the opposite, her body betraying her as she swayed slightly towards him.

Slowly, so slowly, Alessandro leaned forward. His breath fanned Mia's already heated skin as his lips brushed against the knob of her spine and he pressed a lingering kiss to the nape of her neck.

He hadn't meant to do it. Of course he hadn't. Alessandro didn't know what madness had claimed him as he leaned forward and kissed the back of Mia's neck. Everything about the moment felt exquisitely sensual, as if a honeyed drug was stealing through his veins, oblit-erating all rational thought, everything but this. Her.

And he didn't even care.

He felt Mia's instant and overwhelming response, her body shuddering again under his touch, and he moved his lips lower, kissing each knob of her spine in turn, letting his lips linger on her silky skin.

The moonlight turned her ivory skin to lambent sil-ver; she was pale, a perfect goddess, like an ancient marble statue, the paragon of classical beauty. He con-

tinued to kiss his way down her spine, feeling Mia tremble beneath his feather-light touch. Then he reached the
base of her spine and he fell to his knees, anchoring her
hips with his hands, as he kissed the small of her back,
a place he hadn't even considered sensual or enflaming
until this moment, when it was, utterly.

'*Alessandro...*' The name was drawn from her lips
in a desperate plea as the unzipped gown slid from her
hips and pooled around her feet, leaving her completely
bare. She started to turn and Alessandro rose, pulling
her into his arms as his mouth came down hard and
hungry and demanding on hers. She responded to the
kiss with a frenzied passion of her own as they stumbled
backward together, lips locked, hands roving greedily,
until they hit Henry Dillard's desk.

Alessandro hoisted her on top of it, stepping between
her thighs, as he deepened the kiss. He couldn't get
enough of her. He didn't want to. All he wanted was
more—more of this, and more of her.

He broke the kiss only to kiss her elsewhere, wanting to claim all her body for his own—her small, high
breasts, her tiny waist, her endless legs. Mia's head fell
back, her breath coming in desperate pants, as Alessandro explored every inch of her and still felt as if he
hadn't had enough, a thirst and craving welling up inside him that could never be slaked.

He ran his hand from the delicate bones of her ankle
up her calf, along her inner thigh, before his fingers
found the heart of her and she tensed under his touch,
her breath hitching as he deftly stroked her.

'Alessandro…' Another plea, and one he answered with his sure caress.

But even that wasn't enough; it wasn't enough when she surrendered entirely to his touch, her voice a broken, shuddering cry. He needed to possess her fully, to make her his own.

Still, one last shred of sanity made him hesitate. 'Mia, are you sure…?' His voice was low, ragged, but certain. He had to know that she wanted this as much as he did.

Her eyes fluttered open, the look in them both dazed and sated as she nodded, her pulse hammering in her throat. 'Yes,' she whispered. *'Yes.'*

Alessandro needed no further encouragement. He spread her thighs wider as he fumbled with his own clothes. Then seconds, but what felt like an eternity, later he thrust inside her, groaning with the pleasure of it.

Mia let out a startled gasp and Alessandro stilled, shock drenching him in icy waves. 'Mia…' He could barely believe what had just happened. 'Mia, are you…' he could barely manage to say the words '…a *virgin*?'

She let out a choked laugh, her fingernails digging into his shoulders as she anchored him in place. 'I *was*.'

Alessandro swore. 'You…' He bit off what he'd been going to say.

You should have told me. I should have known. I never would have…

He'd *asked*, after all. He'd asked her if she was sure. Now, his body aching and still thundering with need, he started to withdraw.

'No. *Don't.*' Mia clutched his shoulders as she wriggled into position underneath him. 'I'm all right.' She shifted again, her body opening beneath him, inviting him in further, and as Alessandro felt her welcoming warmth he knew he was a lost man. He started to move, and Mia gave a breathy sigh of pleasure as she started to match his rhythm.

The regret and uncertainty he'd felt fell away like a mist as they moved together, climbing higher and higher, until they both reached that dazzling apex, and Alessandro let out a shudder of sated pleasure as he pulled her even closer to him, her body wrapping around and enfolding his. He could feel her heart thudding against his own, and he knew he'd never been as close to another person as this.

Seconds ticked by and neither of them spoke or moved. Alessandro had the strange and unsettling feeling that he didn't *want* to move; he didn't want this to end. He had never, ever felt that way before after being with a woman.

Yet of course he had to, and so did Mia, and after another few soul-shaking seconds she started to pull away. Alessandro let her go, tidying himself up as Mia eased off the desk. Her head was bent, her face averted as she walked quickly to her clothes and pulled them on. Alessandro saw that her fingers trembled as she buttoned the now crumpled white blouse he'd admired earlier that day, in what felt like a lifetime ago.

Alessandro knew he should say something, but he had no idea what. Now that the haze of incredible pleasure was no longer clouding his mind, he was realising what an enormous, idiotic mistake he'd just made. Mia James was his PA, and he'd had her on his desk like a…like a…

No. He could barely believe this had happened. This *never* happened to him, because he never let it. He was too self-controlled, too contained, too certain of what he wanted, to let something as stupid as *desire* cloud his mind and guide his actions, even for a few seconds.

And yet that was precisely what had just happened. He could scarcely credit it, and yet it had. It *had.*

Mia had finished dressing and she stood there, her handbag clutched to her chest, her hair in tangles about her pale face, her eyes wide and dazed.

'I should go.' Her voice was a whisper, and guilty regret lashed him like a whip, which made him, unreasonably he knew, feel angry.

'You should have told me you were a virgin.'

Her already wide eyes widened even further, looking huge in her face. 'Would it have mattered?'

'Yes. I'm not accustomed to…' Alessandro gestured to the desk, unwilling to put it into words, furious with himself as well as with Mia. What had she been thinking? *What had he?*

'Well, obviously neither am I.' Her voice was grim, humourless. 'Let's just say the moment got the better of us, and move past it, shall we?'

He stared at her, surprised and a little discomfited that she was offering so pragmatic an approach, and the one he would have suggested but now oddly resented. Minutes before they'd been twined around each other like…but, no. He wasn't going to think about that. Mia was right. They needed to move past this—immediately.

'Yes.' His voice was tight. 'Yes, that is exactly what we shall do.'

Mia nodded, still looking grim, and Alessandro felt the need to gain control of the situation; somehow it had slipped entirely out of his hands, and he needed to come to grips with it. He needed to remind himself what kind of man he was, and it most certainly wasn't one who unzipped a woman's dress and then ended up having her over a desk in a darkened office.

Those were the actions of a man who had no self-control, no common sense, no sense of containment. They were the actions of a man who allowed lust or any other unruly emotion to control him, and that was not who he was. It couldn't be.

'Are you all right?' he asked stiffly. 'You're not…?' The question nearly brought a blush to his face. He'd never slept with a virgin before. 'You're not hurt?'

'I'm fine,' Mia said flatly. She reached for her coat and shoved her arms in. 'I just need to go home.' She made to leave and Alessandro stayed her with one hand; she flinched under his touch, which both shamed and hurt him.

'Mia, please. Don't leave like this.'

Her eyebrows rose. 'How am I supposed to leave?'

Alessandro didn't know how to answer, couldn't even determine what he wanted. For this never to have happened, he supposed, but there was nothing he could do about that. 'Take the limo,' he said at last. 'It will be safer and quicker.' She stared at him for a moment, her face like a mask, and Alessandro realised how little he was offering. *A lift.* But he didn't know what else he could give her.

'Fine,' she said, and then she shook off his arm and walked out through the door.

CHAPTER FIVE

MIA WOKE UP to bright, wintry sunlight streaming through the window of her bedroom, her head fuzzy and full of cotton wool from the three glasses of champagne she'd had the night before, her body aching in all sorts of unexpected places.

For a single second she simply lay there, enjoying the sunshine, and then memory slammed into her, again and again, as the events of the last evening played in her mind in an unwelcome and humiliating reel.

What had she been *thinking*? During the half-hour ride in Alessandro's limo the night before, she'd been too dazed to truly consider what had happened or its potential consequences, and so she'd simply blanked her mind, stripping off her clothes and falling into bed as soon as she'd returned home, surrendering to the welcome numbness of sleep, except it hadn't claimed her.

She'd tucked her knees up to her chest and scrunched her eyes shut tight, trying to block out the memories that insisted on coming anyway, relentless and so awful. So embarrassing, so full of shame and regret, as well as pleasure and wonder.

She could hardly believe that she'd been so heedless, welcoming Alessandro's kiss, begging him to touch her…and losing her virginity on Henry Dillard's desk. How could she have let that happen? How could she have let herself be so shameless, so *weak*? What if this ruined everything?

Now, in the cold light of morning, she let out a choked sound, something between a sob and a horrified laugh, as she considered what she'd done.

Of course, it had been amazing. There was no denying or hiding from that stark truth. She'd been transported to a world of pleasure she'd never even known existed, and yet, despite that, she hated how in thrall she'd been to her own body, as well as to Alessandro's touch.

He had a hold over her that she both resented and feared, and the result was she'd lost something precious, something that had been hers, in the blazing heat of a single moment…and to a man who most likely didn't like her and intended to fire her in the foreseeable future.

Stupid, stupid, stupid. Stupid and shameful and wrong.

Slowly, still aching, Mia rolled out of bed and headed for the shower, more than ready to wash away the scent of Alessandro from her skin. She turned the water up to as hot as she could stand and let it beat down on her until her skin turned pink and then red.

She knew she needed to get out, get dressed for work, get *going*. She needed to face Alessandro, even if she dreaded it with every cell of her being. Judging from his reaction last night, he regretted their encounter as much as she did, something which was both a relief and an insult. Still, it was better for them to do their best to move past it, and pretend it had never happened… if they could.

Mia felt as if the memory of Alessandro, the strength of his body, the sureness of his touch, was emblazoned on her brain, branded into her skin. It was going to take a huge act of will even to pretend to forget it. *Him*. And yet she had to. The alternative was inconceivable.

Quickly Mia stepped out of the shower and dressed in a crisp skirt suit of navy blue with a pale grey blouse. She put her hair in a tight bun, determined to look every inch the efficient PA and not the kind of woman who had sex late at night in an empty office. Because she wasn't that person. At all.

Since she was eighteen, Mia had been focused on one thing—finding her freedom and forging a career that would give her independence and security. She'd seen how her mother had been miserably beholden to her father throughout their entire marriage, before the release of her death; she'd lived through the awful ups and downs, her father's sudden, inexplicable rages, his emotional blackmail and silent disapproval, his moods and tempers dictating the unhappy tone of their fractured home, and all the while her mother too scared and unsupported to leave.

Diana James had insisted she loved her husband, even when he'd never shown a reason to deserve that love. Mia had been desperate to escape it herself, as soon as she could. And she had vowed she would never lose her control because of a man—any man—the way her mother had. Yet last night, if just for a few moments, she had lost control, willingly, *joyfully*…and she was horrified by it.

Resolutely Mia gazed at her pale reflection in the mirror, determined to put last night behind her completely. Hopefully Alessandro would do the same, and she would return to being the useful PA he required… and nothing more.

The office seemed quiet as Mia headed up in the lift, everyone working quietly with their heads down, seeming apprehensive. Alessandro hadn't started firing people yet, and perhaps if what he'd implied last night was true, he wouldn't.

But who was the real man? The lover who had shown her a hint of vulnerability in his eyes, or the ruthless tycoon everyone said he was? Who did she want to believe in—and did it matter anyway?

At her desk, Mia let out a little sigh of relief as she looked around and didn't see Alessandro anywhere. In an ideal world, she wouldn't see him all day. She could organise the files he'd requested yesterday, and update her CV, just in case. After that, she'd just have to pretend to look busy until Alessandro issued some directives.

As it happened, Mia had barely sat down and clicked on her computer mouse before the lift doors opened and Alessandro strode onto the floor, emanating power and authority in a navy blue suit, looking freshly showered and shaven, reminding Mia of how he'd smelled. Felt.

She tensed where she sat, memories assaulting her senses, and then his steel-grey gaze clashed with hers before he nodded towards the office doors.

'Miss James...?'

Wordlessly Mia rose on rubbery legs and followed him into the office. Her heart was thudding unpleasantly as she closed the door behind her, trying to avoid looking at the desk. Last night when he'd hoisted her up on it, she remembered papers falling, the phone skittering across the polished surface with a clatter. Now, at least, everything had been neatly replaced and there was no way to tell or even guess what had happened there last night.

But Mia remembered. As much as she was trying to forget, she remembered... Alessandro's hands on her hips, her mouth pressed against his shoulder. The way she'd cried out...

Resolutely she looked away from the desk and fixed her gaze on an innocuous spot on the wall. She wasn't ready to look at Alessandro's face and see what expression resided there, derision, desire, or just remembrance. She couldn't handle any of it.

Alessandro cleared his throat. 'Last night...' he began, and then stopped.

Mia reluctantly forced herself to look at him, even though everything in her resisted. His face was bland and closed. She couldn't tell what he was thinking, but she shivered just from the coolness in his eyes.

Last night. The two words did not bode well.

Somehow she forced herself to speak, even though her lips were dry, her voice a papery thread. 'Last night didn't happen.'

'While I'd like to agree with you, I can't.' Alessandro met her gaze unflinchingly. 'We didn't use birth control.'

Shock jolted through Mia at the stark realisation but she kept her gaze and voice steady as she answered. 'I'm on the pill.'

Alessandro raised his eyebrows, seeming sceptical. 'You are? Even though you were a—?'

'Yes.' She cut him off. 'It was to regulate my periods, if you must know.' Except she had, in the welter of her own emotions, forgotten to taken it that morning. And now that she thought about it, with the news of the takeover, she hadn't taken one yesterday either. It had hardly seemed important, considering her lack of a sex life, and yet now...

Mia swallowed hard. Surely skipping just two didn't matter so much? She'd take one later today, in any case. The amount of risk wasn't worth telling Alessandro about. She could not possibly handle his reaction to a potential pregnancy right now. She couldn't get her head around it herself.

'Fine,' Alessandro said. 'It's good to know a pregnancy will not be a concern.'

A pregnancy.

No, she really could not handle thinking about that now. And it was surely so very unlikely. 'No, it is not a concern,' she managed.

'And you do not need to worry about any possible disease,' Alessandro continued steadily, starkly. Something else Mia hadn't even considered, not remotely, although if she'd been thinking straight, she surely would have.

'That's good to know. Thank you.'

They stared at each other, the tension in the room ratcheting up with every second until it felt unbearable. 'Then there's nothing more to say,' Mia said finally, desperate to have this over, to move beyond this moment, and more importantly, beyond last night's moment. 'So, as far as both of us are concerned, last night didn't happen. We can move on as if it didn't. We need to, for the sake of…everything.' She drew herself up, determined to do just that. 'Is there anything you need from me today?'

Alessandro stared at her for a long, hard moment, a muscle ticking in his jaw. 'I'm going to write a letter to all of Dillard's clients,' he said at last. 'You can take it down and then show me a draft copy.'

Mia's heart tumbled in her chest as she felt a weird mix of relief and disappointment that she didn't want to understand. Alessandro was doing what she wanted… trying to act normal. 'Very good,' she said, and turned from the room to get her laptop.

A few minutes later Alessandro was sitting behind his desk and Mia was in front of it, the laptop opened on her knees, her fingers poised on the keyboard, as professional a look as she could manage on her face. This was going to work. She was going to make this work.

She was not going to think about how Alessandro had felt or smelled or tasted, how she'd come apart in his arms and was still desperately trying to put herself together. She wasn't. She absolutely wasn't.

And yet the memories still bombarded her as Alessandro began dictating the letter. It took all her mental power, all her energy and willpower, to focus on the words forming on the screen in front of her instead of what had happened between them last night.

It will get better, Mia told herself. *The memory will fade.*

This was going to work.

This wasn't working.

Alessandro couldn't keep from the glaringly obvious fact as he dictated his letter to Mia. Twice he had to start over, correcting himself, because he was hopelessly distracted by the sight of her, looking as prim and proper as you please, yet still, amazingly, seeming sexy to him.

That tight topknot made him long to pluck the pins from it and run his fingers through the spill of straight, wheat-gold hair. The crisp grey blouse with the mother-of-pearl buttons seemed to be begging to be undone, button by tiny button. The crisp navy suit would look far better crumpled on the floor.

'Mr Costa?' Her voice, crisp and precise, broke into his scattered thoughts. 'You were saying…?'

'I think, considering the circumstances, you should call me Alessandro.'

Something sparked in her eyes. 'I do not wish to consider the circumstances, and I didn't think you did, either.'

'I meant,' Alessandro clarified, 'as your employer.' But he hadn't been thinking of her as his employee. Not at all.

A faint pink touched Mia's cheeks, making her look

all the more delectable. Making him want her all the more. 'Of course,' she murmured, and turned towards back to her laptop, her gaze focused determinedly on the screen.

Alessandro went back to dictating the letter, but again he lost his train of thought, which infuriated him. This was *not* who he was. This was not who he could be.

'Mr... Alessandro?' Mia prompted. Again. Her eyebrows were raised, her eyes so very blue.

'Type up what you have,' Alessandro said abruptly. 'And I'll look at it then. Thank you.'

Wordlessly Mia nodded, rising from her seat in one elegantly fluid movement. Alessandro couldn't keep from watching her as she left the room, noting her long, slim legs in sheer tights, the low navy pumps. As far as he was concerned, she could have been wearing a negligee and stiletto heels. Her staid, puritanical outfit still enflamed him, and that was most definitely a problem.

The door clicked shut softly behind her, and Alessandro swivelled in his chair, too restless to get back to his work, although he certainly had plenty to do. He needed to weed through Dillard's clients and decided which ones were worth keeping. He needed to woo the clients he wanted to stay on and make sure that they did. And he needed to find positions for the employees he intended on keeping, and offer redundancy packages to the ones he didn't.

Which made him think of Mia. He'd intended on keeping her in the office for at least another week, to help smooth the transition period, but that thought felt like torture now. He could at least check on the details for her eventual transfer, to make sure it happened as easily and quickly as possible.

He was always generous with his offers, and so he would be with Mia. It made the most sense. It filled him with relief, that he could be proactive about arranging her inevitable transfer. All it would take were a few phone calls.

Alessandro felt his shoulders loosen at the thought of being free of this alarming obsession he'd developed—and over someone so unprepossessing. He'd been with women, *many* women, who were far more attractive and alluring than Mia James, with her straight hair and English schoolgirl looks. What was it about her that affected him so much, drove him to such irritating distraction?

It didn't matter. His involvement with Mia James was thankfully going to come to an end. He was just reaching for the phone to make the first call when a knock sounded on the door.

'Yes?' he barked.

'It's Miss… Mia. May I speak to you?'

After a second's hesitation he put the phone down. 'Come in.'

She slipped into the office, her blue eyes looking crystal-bright as she met his gaze, a hint of determined challenge to the tilt of her chin.

'I wanted to speak to you.'

'About?'

She angled her chin a bit higher. 'I'd like to request a transfer.'

Shock rooted him to the spot, the phone dangling from his hand. 'A what?'

'A transfer. I don't think it is prudent for us to work together. You mentioned that you found positions for your employees when possible, so I'm asking for you to find me one.' Her eyes blazed as they met his. 'Somewhere preferably not in London.'

She wanted to be shot of him, Alessandro realised dazedly. Just as he wanted to be shot of her...so why did the thought rankle so much?

'Where is this coming from?' he asked, even though he knew. Of course he knew.

'Where do you think?' she returned sharply. 'You mentioned my usefulness as your PA would only be for so long.'

'But it's not finished yet,' he returned, surprised and a bit alarmed by his own annoyance. He'd been planning this very thing, and yet absurdly he resented her suggesting it first.

'I think it is finished,' Mia answered levelly, her tone brooking no disagreement. And, despite the instinctive, gut-level reaction that he had to argue with her, even to insist that she stay, Alessandro held his tongue. Mia wanted what he wanted. Surely he wasn't so pigheaded as to resist simply because it was now her idea rather than his?

'There are two possibilities, actually,' he said after a moment. 'I was looking into them myself, for this very eventuality.'

'I'm sure you were,' Mia returned dryly and Alessandro had the uncomfortable feeling she'd known what he'd been thinking, and had simply pre-empted him. 'The first is as personal assistant to the CEO of the Arras Hotel Group, based in Los Angeles,' he said. 'It's a property company I acquired two years ago, running luxury hotels on America's west coast.'

'Los Angeles…' She nodded slowly. 'And the other?'

'Personal assistant to the CEO of a tech company in Sweden. Or, if you prefer, you can take the standard redundancy package. You'll find I'm very generous.'

'I'm sure.'

'I'll get you the details of both positions.' He leaned down to his laptop, and a few clicks later he'd printed it all out and handed Mia the pages.

She took them calmly, scanning them with a cool composure that somehow rattled him.

'Both positions come with accommodation provided, and the salary is fifty percent higher than yours was here,' he felt compelled to point out.

'And I can start immediately?'

She couldn't wait to leave, could she? 'If you like. Of course, you can have some time to pack up and arrange your travel. All paid for, naturally.'

'Naturally.' She glanced at the paper again. 'I choose Los Angeles,' she said firmly, although underneath that conviction he heard a tremble to her voice that unnerved him. He almost told her that she didn't need to do this, but of course she did. If not now, then next week, or the week after that. Better for her to feel it was on her terms.

'I'm sure you'll be very happy there,' he said as equably as he could manage. 'Good luck with your move.'

She stared at him for a moment, her lips twisting and then tightening. 'I'll clear my desk, then,' she said, which made it sound as if she'd been fired.

'You don't have to do—' Alessandro began, and she gave him a piercing look.

'I think it's better this way, don't you?'

Yes, he did. Of course he did. Even if he didn't feel like it just then. 'Enjoy LA,' he said stiffly, and she gave him one last accusing look before she nodded and walked out of the room.

CHAPTER SIX

THREE WEEKS AFTER she'd left Alessandro Costa, Dillard Investments, and her home country, Mia came home from work, unlocking the door to her sumptuous apartment in Santa Monica, one of Los Angeles' best neighbourhoods, with a tired sigh as she kicked off her heels.

Choosing to transfer workplaces had been the only way she'd known how to salvage what was left of her pride as well as her working life. She hadn't been able to stand working with Alessandro, and in any case she'd sensed that he would have her transferred or even fired if she'd waited long enough; she was no longer *useful* in the way he required. In fact, she'd become rather inconvenient. Choosing it herself first had felt like the best way to take control.

Since she'd left she'd heard through the grapevine that at least half of Dillard's employees had been made redundant with packages as generous as hers; the other half had been offered positions within Alessandro's portfolio of companies. He wasn't the ruthless tycoon she'd thought he was, at least not in that regard.

It was just in his personal relationships where he was truly ruthless. Because no matter how elegant her apartment, how cushy her job, Mia couldn't escape the feeling that Alessandro had wanted her gone, more even than she'd wanted to go. She hadn't seen him since the day she'd walked out of her office, which was how she'd wanted it—and how Alessandro had seemed to want it, as well.

Sighing, she changed out of her work clothes into more comfy ones, anticipating another evening in front of the TV. She'd been invited out for drinks with some of her colleagues, but for the last few days Mia had been feeling a bit off, tired and nauseous. She hoped she wasn't coming down with the stomach flu, and decided that a good night's sleep, not to mention a healthy dose of Netflix, would knock whatever she was fighting off on its head.

The next morning she woke up with her stomach roiling, and she barely made it to the toilet in time before it emptied its contents. She called in sick, although by the afternoon she was feeling better again. When the same thing happened the next day, and then the next day after that, realisation sliced through her, as sharp as a knife, and just as shockingly painful, even though she'd known all along it had been an admittedly small risk.

She hadn't had a period since she'd come to Los Angeles. Sick in the mornings, better in the afternoons, and so, so tired. She might have been a virgin, but she wasn't completely naïve.

She'd missed two birth control pills, and even though

she'd taken one later that day, Mia had read online that she'd opened herself up to a small risk of becoming pregnant. And a small risk was still a risk.

Yet even so, she had trouble believing it.

One night. Two pills. Surely not...

Her heart turned over, an unpleasant sensation, as realisation trickled icily through her.

She couldn't be...

After work that day she went to the nearest pharmacy to buy a pregnancy test, flushing in embarrassment as she paid for it, even though the pimply-faced teenaged boy ringing up her purchase looked completely bored and indifferent.

She took it home, unwrapping it with shaking fingers, staring at the slim white stick in disbelief that she was holding such a thing, needing it.

She couldn't be...

She read the directions twice through, still in a haze of incredulity, and then she took the test, all the while telling herself this was crazy, impossible, nothing more than a needless precaution. The chances of falling pregnant after one time, and just two missed pills...

But she wasn't stupid. She knew it could happen. She just couldn't believe it could happen to her.

And then she turned the test over and stared down at the two blazing pink lines in disbelief.

She couldn't be, but she was.

She spent an hour simply sitting on her sofa, staring into space, having no idea what to think, much less to do. Her mind felt fogged with incredulity, unable to think beyond the reality of those two lines. She couldn't yet consider what they meant or would mean, or how she would respond to them.

Then, at some point, she roused herself from her stupor and made herself a cup of tea. Pregnant. She was pregnant. By Alessandro Costa, a man she barely knew and definitely didn't like, a man known to be ruthless in both personal relationships and the business world. And he was going to be the father of her child.

Realisation slammed into her with that thought; this was her *child*. The family she'd never truly had. And she knew, no matter how inconvenient or unexpected, she was going to keep this baby, this child of her flesh and blood.

And Alessandro's.

Armed with a cup of milky tea, Mia flipped open her laptop and did another internet search on Alessandro. She had deliberately not searched anything personal about him before. She hadn't wanted to know, or to wonder.

Now she blinked as image after image came up on the screen of her laptop of Alessandro. The sight of his commanding profile, those steely eyes, that impressive form…it all battered her senses, made her remember far too many things. The lingering way he'd undone her zip. The press of his lips to the base of her spine…the sudden frenzy of passion they'd both felt, obliterating all thought and reason for those few crucial moments.

As she clicked through the photos, she noticed a common feature, and her expression hardened. In nearly every image, Alessandro was with a woman. A different woman. Over the last month he'd attended a variety of glittering events, in London, in Paris, in Rome, always with a sexy, pouting woman, and usually one who was poured into a dress, on his arm. Clearly he'd completely forgotten about her.

She pushed the laptop away and took a sip of her tea, feeling sick in a way that had nothing to do with the tiny being she nurtured in her womb. That man—that ruthless, arrogant, philandering man—was her baby's father. And she knew she would have to tell him so.

She shuddered with dread at the thought of Alessandro's reaction. Disbelief? Displeasure? He was not going to be pleased, of that Mia was completely certain. And, judging by the way he handled hostile takeovers, he was going to expect Mia to fall in with his plans, whatever they would be.

And what *would* they be? Would he want to, heaven forbid, get rid of their child, considering him or her an inconvenience he couldn't abide? Or would he throw money at her, to make her go away? She knew he would want to do something, but she had no idea what it would be.

And what did *she* want? Never to see Alessandro Costa again, preferably. Perhaps he wanted the same thing. Hopefully they could come to an agreement, even if this wasn't a scenario either of them had envisioned or wanted.

Of course, she had to get in touch with him first, and Mia didn't really know how to do that. She'd never had his personal information and she certainly wasn't going to find it online. The best she could hope for was to call the headquarters of Costa International and hope the message was passed on. After that…it was surely up to him. The thought comforted her. All she could do was try, surely.

The next morning, Mia made the call to Costa International in Rome, and got the switchboard.

'I'd like to speak to Alessandro Costa, please.' She tried to make her voice sound confident and firm, and had a feeling she failed.

'I'm afraid he's not available.'

'This is important and personal. Is there another number on which I could reach him?'

'I'm afraid not.'

Mia bit her lip, fighting both frustration and a treacherous relief. *She'd tried…* 'Then may I leave a message?' she asked, and the receptionist's voice was toneless as she answered.

'Of course.'

'And can I be sure it will get to him?' Mia pressed, determined to make a good effort. 'It's important.'

'Of course.'

She left her name and number. 'Please do give him the message,' she said, knowing she was probably annoying the receptionist but needing, as a matter of principle, to communicate the urgency of the matter. 'It's important.'

'He'll get the message,' the receptionist assured her in a bored voice, and then disconnected the call.

Mia sat back, feeling the tiniest bit relieved. She'd made the effort. She'd tried to be in touch. If Alessandro didn't get the message…

Guilt needled her at the thought. She knew she could

ask her boss for his personal details, although whether he'd be willing to give them out, she didn't know. Still, she supposed she could try harder.

But the grim truth was, she didn't want to. She knew what it was like to be controlled by a man, someone who dictated what she wore and ate and did. Her father had done all of the above, simply because he could. Mia had lost track of the times he'd insisted she change her clothes, or told her she couldn't go out, or insisted the dinner her mother had made was inedible when it had been fine. Her entire childhood had been one of barely endured oppression, and she could not bear the thought of opening herself up to that again.

Alessandro might not be as odiously domineering as her father, but already in their short relationship he'd told her what to do, what to wear, where to go. It was obvious to Mia that he was someone who liked being in control, not just of his employees, but everyone in his life. And she could not let him be in control of her, or her child. Not like that.

She'd *tried*. She'd left a message, she'd said it was important. And that, Mia told herself, pushing away the guilt that still pricked her, was all she could do.

A year later

He hadn't meant to look her up. He'd excised her from his mind and memory, or done his very best to, even if some nights he still woke up with dreams of her lingering in his mind like an enticing mist, making him remember. Making him want.

In his waking hours, he thought of her not at all, an act of sheer, determined will, and yet, a year later, as he returned to the office of Dillard Investments that he'd done his best to avoid for the last twelve months, he realised some part of him had been thinking of her all along.

Alessandro had worked hard this last year to incorporate Dillard's clients and assets into his ever-increasing portfolio. He hadn't been back to London in all that time, but now, with another recent British acquisition under his belt, he had needed to return to the former office of Dillard Investments, now part of Costa International.

As he strode through Henry Dillard's old office he tried not to look at *that* desk. Yet even when he was determinedly not looking at it, he was remembering. Remembering Mia's innocent and yet overwhelming response, the way her body had clasped his in complete embrace and surrender. The dazed look in her eyes afterwards, the way her fingers had fumbled as she'd buttoned her blouse. And the next day, when she'd asked for a transfer before he'd been able to order it himself.

A year on, Alessandro could reluctantly acknowledge that perhaps he should have taken a bit more care with Mia's rather abrupt transfer. And now she was on the other side of the world, admittedly by her own choice, but he hadn't even checked whether she'd settled in or was enjoying her job.

It would be the right thing, Alessandro mused, to check on her, just to see how she was doing, that she was enjoying Los Angles and her position with the Arras Hotel Group.

He wouldn't have to talk to her; she wouldn't even have to know. He could ask Eric Foster, the CEO of the Arras Group, a man he'd put in place to run the half-dozen exclusive hotels located on the west coast of America that he'd taken over five years ago. This was nothing more than a courtesy call, a way to clear his conscience…if it needed clearing in the first place.

And yet, as he dialled the number, he felt his heart rate quicken. What if he was put through to Mia herself? What if she was happy to hear from him?

As if, on both counts. He was a fool for thinking it, for wanting it even a little.

'Mia James?' Foster sounded surprised when Alessandro mentioned her. 'She was working out wonderfully, of course. I knew she would, if you'd recommended her.'

'Was?' Alessandro frowned, a sense of unease clenching his gut. 'Isn't she still working for you?'

'Not at the moment.' Taylor let out a little laugh that Alessandro didn't understand. 'She stopped about three months ago, but she's expecting to be back this summer, no pun intended.' He let out another laugh, and Alessandro's frown deepened, his body tensing.

No pun…? What was that supposed to mean? 'Has something happened to make her take such a leave of absence?'

'Has something happened?' Taylor repeated, sounding surprised. 'I guess you don't know…no reason why you would, although I thought she was a personal friend of yours…'

'Know what?' Alessandro demanded, brushing the man's other words aside. He was not about to explain his relationship, or lack of it, to Mia James in any detail whatsoever.

'Sorry, sorry. She's on maternity leave. She had a baby three months ago. A little girl.'

For a second Alessandro couldn't speak. Couldn't think. He felt as if his brain were short-circuiting, misfiring. *A baby.* A baby three months ago…nine months after their night together.

It was impossible. *Impossible.* She'd been on the pill. She would have told him. Surely, no matter what had or hadn't happened between them, she would have told him. *It couldn't be…*

'Right, I must have forgotten that.' His voice, attempting joviality, sounded forced. 'Of course.'

'I hope she comes back,' Taylor said. 'She's a good PA. The best I've ever had.'

'Yes.' Alessandro's mind felt as if it was buzzing, full of static and white noise. He could not form a single coherent thought. 'Yes,' he said again, and then he disconnected the call. He flung the phone across his desk, glad when it clattered noisily across the surface. He half wished it would break, that something would, because he realised he was furious.

Furious, because Mia James might have had his baby and not even told him. Not *ever* told him. His fists clenched as his blood pumped through his body in hectic, vengeful thuds. How dared she? *How dared she?* To

not tell him something so critical, so utterly important...
To deprive him of knowing his own child...

Unless it wasn't his child?

A little girl. His mind raced as he paced the confines
of the room like something caged. Could it be another
man's? Yet she'd been a virgin, no other men in the picture as far as he knew, but of course he *didn't* know...
anything. And yet he couldn't believe Mia would have
gone with another man so soon after. Surely it was his.
Surely...

There was only one way to find out.

He took his private jet to Los Angeles that night,
cancelling half a dozen meetings without a word of
explanation. The flight felt endless, his mind going in
pointless circles as he considered what he would say
to Mia.

If it was his child, his daughter, then he knew what
he wanted, and he knew he'd do anything, *anything*,
to see it happen. He'd grown up without a father, and
it had tormented him for all his childhood. He would
never, ever allow a child of his to experience that same
sense of loss, confusion, and grief. He'd never walk
away from his own flesh and blood the way his father
had, without a single thought or care.

But perhaps the baby wasn't his. A thought that, ir-
rationally, gave him a little lurch of disappointment,
even as he recognised that his treatment of Mia had
been less than admirable. Could he really blame her if
she'd met someone else and forgotten him?

A limo picked him up at the airport and drove him to
the address of Mia's apartment that he'd had on file. It

was a beautiful, balmy evening, the sun setting over the ocean, its placid surface shimmering with crimson and gold, palm trees silhouetted against a darkening sky.

The apartment building where Mia lived was a two-storey stucco house with an apartment on each floor and a pool in the back. Hers was on the second floor, and he mounted the steps with grim determination. Rapped once, short and hard. Waited.

A few seconds later he heard light footsteps, and then the slip of a chain before the door opened. Mia stood there, the questioning smile on her face morphing into an expression of complete and utter shock.

'Alessandro…' His name came out in a whisper.

'You should have told me.' The words came out before he could stop them.

Her face paled and one hand fluttered to her throat. 'How did you…?'

'So it is mine?' he interjected grimly, and her eyes sparked.

'It is a she, which you probably already know, considering you're here.'

'Yes, I do.' He'd forgotten her fire, and how it annoyed and impressed him in equal measure. 'Are you going to let me in?'

Wordlessly she stepped aside, closing the door behind him. Alessandro looked around the room, noting its bland corporate furnishings softened by familial touches—a colourful mat and baby's activity gym on the floor, a pink bouncy seat in one corner, a wicker basket of bright toys by the coffee table.

He turned to Mia, taking in how she had changed.

Her hair was pulled back loosely, golden tendrils framing a rounder, softer face. Her figure was rounder and softer too, more womanly. She was dressed in a tunic top and capris, casual clothes he realised he'd never seen her in. Of course, he'd barely seen her at all. He'd known her for two days. Two short, incredible, life-changing days.

Neither of them spoke; she regarded him nervously, wiping her palms down the sides of her flowing top.

'Where is she?' he demanded.

'Sleeping in her nursery. Alessandro…'

'You should have told me.' He couldn't get past that. 'No matter what did or didn't happen between us, you should have told me.' He shook his head. 'I can't forgive that, Mia.'

'You can't *forgive*?' Her nervousness fell away as she stared at him incredulously. 'You have some cheek, Alessandro Costa.'

Now he was glaring as well, both of them with daggers drawn, only moments into their meeting. 'What is that supposed to mean?'

'What makes you think I didn't try to tell you?' She planted her hands on her hips, her eyes furious slits of bright, bright blue. 'Why do you *assume*?'

He shook his head slowly. He wasn't buying that. 'If you'd tried, I would have known.'

'Oh, really? You, the head of a huge, sprawling multibillion-dollar organisation? You think a message from a nobody PA would have been passed on?'

He frowned. 'So how did you try to reach me?'

'The only way I knew how,' she snapped. 'Through the switchboard of Costa International.'

His frown deepened, but he still couldn't concede the point. 'There must have been a better way...'

'And what way would that have been?' Mia challenged. Now she was the one who sounded angry and aggrieved, the one who was in the right, and yet Alessandro felt she couldn't be. *She couldn't be.* 'You didn't exactly want to keep in touch, did you? I didn't have any of your contact details, and I was under the distinct impression you never wanted to lay eyes on me again. Which was fine by me, because I didn't want to lay eyes on you.'

Which, absurdly, stung, even though he knew it shouldn't have. It wasn't as if they'd had a relationship, or even been friends. 'A baby changes things, obviously,' he snapped. 'A baby changes everything.'

CHAPTER SEVEN

MIA STARED AT ALESSANDRO, a feeling of dread surging along with the anger that had been her instinctive response, even though she knew he had a point. For the last year she'd been fighting a sense of guilt over the fact that she hadn't tried harder to tell him, but she'd always justified it to herself, telling herself at least she had tried to give him a message, and in any case he wouldn't have cared anyway. Presumptions, she realised now, that were utterly wrong, because Alessandro looked as if he cared very much indeed.

Now he was standing there in front of her, she felt overwhelmed by the sheer presence of him, too dazed to hold on to a single coherent thought. When she'd seen him at her door, she'd felt the blood rush from her head, and she'd had to clutch the doorframe to keep herself upright.

She'd never thought she'd see Alessandro again. She'd convinced herself that he would never find out, that he'd never look for her, that he'd never care. Clearly she'd been wrong.

Several times she'd wondered about making more of

an effort to let him know he was going to be a father, but she'd never felt brave enough, and as the months had gone on and on it had felt harder and harder to do.

Once Ella had been born, she'd been too tired and overwhelmed to think about Alessandro at all, much less worry about him.

But now he was here, looking furious and wronged, and she had no idea what to do about it. After everything she'd been through—terrible morning sickness, a difficult labour and delivery, and Ella's colicky start to life—she didn't think she could handle Alessandro's outrage on top of it.

'I'm sorry,' she said as she did her best to stand her ground and meet his stony gaze. 'But I did try to reach you.'

'So what are you saying?' Alessandro demanded. 'You left a message with the switchboard saying you were having my baby?' He sounded scathing.

'No, of course not,' Mia answered with dignity. 'I would never be so indiscreet, especially concerning a matter so personal to both of us. I simply said it was urgent and very important that you receive my message, and I asked you to return my call. Which you never did.'

'Because I never got the message!' Alessandro exploded. 'As you very well should have been able to guess.'

Mia drew a steadying breath. 'That is not my fault, Alessandro.'

'No?' Alessandro shook his head slowly. 'Surely there were other ways, Mia. You could have told your boss, Eric Foster. He has my details. You could have got them from him, and contacted me directly.'

Mia looked away, knowing she could have done exactly that. Guilt needled her again, sharp, painful pricks. 'To be honest, Alessandro, I didn't think you'd care.'

The silence that met this statement was thunderous. Alessandro stared at her, his mouth open, his eyes flinty, before he folded his arms across his impressive chest and raked her with a single, scathing glare. 'You didn't *think*? Or you didn't want to know? You hid my own child from me—'

'Yes, I did,' Mia cried. 'I felt I had to.'

'Why?'

'Because…because I was scared.' She hated admitting it, but she didn't know what else to do.

'What were you scared of?'

'You. Sweeping into my life, making demands.'

'Like seeing my own child? Is that such an outrageous demand?'

'I was afraid you might ask for something else,' Mia admitted in a low voice. Alessandro's eyes narrowed to deadly slits.

'Ask for something else…?'

'A termination,' she admitted, unable to look at him as she said it. 'You didn't seem thrilled about a potential pregnancy when you mentioned it to me…' She trailed off, because the absolutely outraged look on Alessandro's face kept her from any speech or thought. She shrank beneath his anger, hating that she was doing so.

She'd promised herself never to cower or cringe, and yet here she was, doing both.

'A termination,' Alessandro said, and then swore. 'How dare you make such decisions for me?'

It seemed a strange twist of irony that in trying not to be controlled, she had come across as controlling. Mia sank onto the sofa, overwhelmed by Alessandro's anger, by the way everything had been turned upside down.

'I'm sorry,' she said in a low voice. 'I see now that I shouldn't have. You just seemed so alarmed by the possibility of a pregnancy…'

'And you assured me you couldn't be pregnant! You were on the pill.'

'I was, but I missed two, because of…well, because of everything.'

'And you didn't think to tell me that? To alert me to the possibility?'

'It seemed such a tiny risk…'

'Obviously not.' He wheeled away from her, his anger making him need to move. 'You made decisions you had no right to make.'

'I thought I was doing what was best. And it isn't as if you were checking up or even thinking of me all year, were you?' she flung at him, tired of being on the defensive. 'I did an internet search on you, you know. And I have to tell you, Alessandro, what I saw made me less inclined to search you out.'

Alessandro turned back to her, his powerful body taut and still. 'What you *saw*?'

'It looked like you were with a different woman every night.' Mia lifted her chin. 'Supermodels and socialites, by the look of them. Your bedroom must have a revolving door.'

'You almost sound jealous,' Alessandro remarked in a low, dangerous tone.

'Hardly,' Mia scoffed. 'But from what I saw, you didn't seem like father material.' As soon as she said the words, she knew she'd gone too far. Something dark and deadly thrummed through Alessandro, tautening his body, flaring in his eyes.

'You are not in a position to judge my parenting skills,' he said in a voice that was all the more frightening in its quiet intensity. 'That was not your right, just as it was not your right to keep this information—and my own child—from me.' Mia opened her mouth, trying to frame a response that was not quite an apology, but Alessandro cut across her before she'd barely drawn a breath. 'In any case, whatever you saw online...those were nothing more than social engagements.'

'Are you saying it never went further?' she scoffed. 'I have trouble believing—'

'I'm not saying one thing or the other,' Alessandro replied, his voice rising, edged with ire. 'It has no relevance. We weren't a couple. *I didn't know.*' He took a step towards her, menacing in his stature, his pure physical presence. Mia held her ground, but only just. 'No matter what photos you saw of me online, you should have told me I was going to be a father. *End of.*'

'Fine.' Her voice quavered as her hands once more bunched into helpless fists at her sides. 'Fine, I should have. I admit that. But...can't you admit your part in this? Getting rid of me the day after...' Her voice trembled and broke. 'The very next day, Alessandro. Can't you realise how that made me feel?'

Colour slashed his cheekbones as he jerked his head in a brief nod. 'It would have happened eventually, but I admit, our…liaison precipitated it. I thought working together would be a distraction. Perhaps I shouldn't have been quite so…abrupt.'

'So that was you making a unilateral decision,' Mia returned, her voice shaking, 'while calling me to account for doing the same.'

'They're entirely different situations, Mia. A job versus a baby. You cannot compare,' Alessandro fired back, taking another step towards her so they were nearly standing toe to toe. Mia felt exhausted by his anger; her daughter was three months old, she'd been going it alone the entire time, and she was hormonal and sleep deprived and very near tears. Still, she took a steadying breath and met his furious, narrowed gaze with a challenging one of her own.

'I'm not comparing, I'm only asking you to understand where I was coming from.'

'I can't understand at all where you're coming from,' he snapped. 'What you did was inexcusable—'

'Did you come here to blame me, Alessandro, for everything? Because I get it. This is all my fault. Message received. Now you can go home.' Her voice trembled and tears she was desperate for him not to see stung her eyes. She turned away from him, too tired to keep battling.

She flopped onto the sofa, tucking her knees up to her chest. She'd just put Ella down for a nap and she'd been hoping for a little sleep herself. Clearly that was now an impossibility, which alone was enough to make her cry.

'I'm not going home.' Alessandro came to sit on the sofa opposite her, his hands resting on his knees. He gave her a level look that Mia could barely summon the energy to return.

'What do you want, then?' she asked tiredly, only to realise how open and dangerous that question was.

Now that she could think about it all properly, the shock of seeing him finally starting to fade, she realised he'd flown a long way for nothing more than a confrontation. He couldn't have come simply for that. He had to want more. A lot more. But what?

'I want my daughter,' Alessandro stated simply, the words icing the blood in her veins and freezing her soul. She stared at him, as trapped as an animal in a snare, as his iron-hard gaze slammed into hers. 'And I'm not leaving without her.'

Alessandro hadn't meant the words as a threat, but he recognised that they sounded like one. He saw it in the flare of Mia's eyes, the pulse that beat in her throat, as her hand crept up to press against her chest as if to still her fast-thudding heart. No, it wasn't a threat. It was a promise.

'Alessandro, be reasonable…'

'Reasonable? What is reasonable about having my child hidden from me for three months—?'

'I didn't *hide*.' Her voice trembled but he still heard a note of quiet dignity in it that struck an emotional chord within him. 'Please, Alessandro, for…for our daughter's sake, can we not play the blame game? Surely we can reach some kind of…of arrangement…'

An *arrangement*?

Was she hoping to fob him off with some half-baked idea of shared custody, parental visitations? 'The only arrangement I'm interested in,' Alessandro told her curtly, 'is to take my daughter back to where she belongs.'

Mia's eyes looked huge and dark in her face. 'Which is where?'

'Home. My villa in Tuscany. It is the perfect place to raise a child.' As he said the words, he knew how much he meant them. His daughter would not have the kind of chaotic, unstable childhood he'd had, filled with strangers and strange places. She would have every need provided for, emotional *and* physical. And that required a home, with two parents fully involved in her life. He would not negotiate on any of those points, as a matter of principle and honour.

Mia pressed her lips together; Alessandro saw the sheen of tears in her eyes, giving them a luminous quality. 'And what are you expecting me to do? Just…just hand her over?'

It took Alessandro a moment to realise what she thought, what she'd assumed—that he would take their daughter, and leave her here. Did she really think him such a monster? Had she thought he'd been threatening *that*? He felt both hurt and shamed by the idea.

'No, of course not. I would never ask or expect such a thing. A child belongs with her mother as well as her father, especially one as young as ours.' *Ours.* A ripple of shock went through him at the thought; he had a *child.* They did. He still couldn't grasp it fully, the implications crashing over him in endless waves.

'Then…' Mia's worried gaze scanned his face. 'You want me to go with you?' She sounded as if she could scarcely credit such a possibility.

'Yes, of course I do.' It had been obvious to Alessandro from the beginning, considering his own unfortunate background, and one he would never, ever wish on a child of his own. A child belonged with his or her parents. Always.

He could see now from Mia's stunned expression that she had not considered that. No wonder she'd been so hostile; she thought he'd been going to *steal* their child, as if he'd ever do such a despicable thing.

Mia shook her head slowly. 'Go with you…to Tuscany?' she clarified, as if she still couldn't believe it.

'Yes.'

'But…' Mia continued to shake her head, as if she could not imagine such a thing coming to pass.

'There is surely nothing keeping you here,' Alessandro observed. 'You've only lived here a year.'

'As you know so well,' she returned.

'So I fail to see any problem.'

'You just expect me to—to *uproot* myself yet again…'

'For our child.' As if on cue, a faint cry sounded through the flat, making them both still and stare at each other. The moment spun on, both of them frozen, and then she cried again. *His daughter.* 'Where… where is she…?' Alessandro began, barely able to form the words.

Wordlessly Mia rose from the sofa and went down

the hallway to the flat's bedrooms. Alessandro followed, his heart starting to thud. *His daughter.*

'Hello, darling.' Mia's voice had softened into an unfamiliar coo as she opened the door to a small bedroom decked out in pale grey and mint green. Alessandro stood in the doorway, transfixed, as Mia went to the cot and bent over it, then scooped up the tiny form that had been inside.

She turned to Alessandro, the baby pressed to her shoulder, one hand cradling her head possessively. She was *tiny*, a mere scrap of humanity, and so very precious, bundled in a white velveteen sleepsuit.

'This is Ella.' Mia's voice trembled. 'Do you…do you want to hold her?'

Hold her?

Alarm warred with a deep longing. Alessandro stared at her for a moment, speechless and uncertain for what felt like the first time in his life.

Did he want to hold her? *Yes.*

Was he terrified? *Yes.*

He nodded, not trusting himself to speak, not sure what to do. How did one hold a baby? He had no idea. He had never held one before.

Mia walked towards him, still cradling their daughter. *Ella.* She came to stand in front of him, close enough that Alessandro was able to breathe in her achingly familiar scent of understated citrus. It assaulted his senses and made him remember far too many things.

'Hold your arms out,' Mia instructed, and Alessandro thrust both arms out stiffly in front of him. 'Not like that,' she said with a small smile, a surprising and strangely gratifying trace of laughter in her voice.

'How?' Alessandro demanded. 'I don't know what to do.' This was a vulnerability he couldn't hide. Knowledge he had never possessed.

'Like this.' Gently, holding Ella with one arm, she guided Alessandro's own, manipulating his limbs as if he were a mannequin, until one arm was bent as if to cradle a football, the other arm to support it. 'Now we just add the baby,' she said softly, and before he knew what she was doing, she put Ella into his arms.

He cradled her to him instinctively, pressing her tiny body gently against his chest as she snuffled into his neck. He breathed in the sweet, milky warmth of her as his heart contracted, expanded, and contracted again. He *felt*. It hurt.

'That's the way,' Mia encouraged him. 'You've got the hang of it now.'

He felt like a complete novice, inexperienced, incapable, and if he were holding the most fragile and yet explosive thing possible—a cross between a stick of dynamite and a Ming vase.

'I don't want to hurt her,' he confessed, undone by this child in his arms, this fragile, precious, *impossible* human being.

'You aren't hurting her,' Mia assured him. Tears sparkled in her eyes and she blinked them back rapidly. 'Trust me, she would let you know if you were.'

'Does she cry? Is she...is she a good baby?' He realised how much he wanted to know—all the details, all he'd missed. It didn't matter now that he'd missed them or why he had, he just wanted to *know*.

'She's a wonderful baby, but she's had her moments.' The smile Mia gave him was weary, and he suddenly noticed how tired she looked. Realised how hard it must have been, to parent alone all these months… which was all the more reason for her to come to Tuscany with him, where she could have help, and comfort, and space.

'You'll come to Tuscany,' he said, and it sounded like an order. Mia's gentle, tired smile faltered as a familiar fire sparked in her eyes.

'Alessandro, you can't order me about…'

'You'll come,' he insisted. 'And Ella, too. You must.' His voice was too strident, his manner too abrupt and autocratic. He knew that, and yet he couldn't keep himself from it, because it was so very important. It was everything.

He saw the remoteness enter Mia's eyes, felt her coolness as she took Ella out of his arms, pressing her against her shoulder as she half turned away from him.

'She needs a feed,' she murmured, but it felt like an excuse. She slipped past him and went back to the main living area, leaving Alessandro no choice but to follow.

When he came into the room, Mia was sitting back on the sofa, Ella brought to her breast, one tiny fist clutching a tendril of golden hair. Shock jolted through him at the sight of her feeding their daughter, the simple, pure *rightness* of it, followed by a rush of primal possessiveness that nearly felled him with its intensity, its sureness.

This was his *family.* The family he'd never had himself, the family he hadn't even realised he wanted. And he was never letting them go.

CHAPTER EIGHT

MIA WATCHED THE streets of Los Angeles stream by in a colourful blur as the limousine Alessandro had called for her sped towards his luxury hotel in the downtown area of the city. After leaving abruptly the day before, when Mia had begun feeding Ella, he'd commanded she come to where he was staying to discuss their future arrangements…whatever those might be.

Mia had spent a sleepless night, wide-eyed and worried, trying to decide how she was going to respond to Alessandro's suggestion that she move to Tuscany with Ella. Everything in her resisted that notion, and particularly the high-handed manner in which he'd delivered it, as if he expected her to fall in with his plans without so much as a whisper of dissent.

She did not want to be controlled by him, and yet she feared she had no choice. Just like with her father, Alessandro was calling the shots. Just like her father, he had all the power, all the money, all the cards. It had taken years from Mia to break free from her father. She desperately wanted to have the strength to break free from Alessandro now, even as she recognised that Alessandro was a different man from her father, and she'd sensed a kindness beneath his hard exterior that made her want to trust him.

Still, it wasn't enough to move continents for, surely.

And yet... Ella. She couldn't deny Alessandro the right to see his daughter. After witnessing him holding Ella, the obvious love in his eyes, surprising and powerful, she didn't even want to. So where did that leave her? *Them?*

In the car seat next to her, Ella stirred, blinking wide blue-grey eyes at the world, her thumb finding its way to her mouth, a new discovery. Mia gazed down at her infant daughter, her heart squeezing painfully with love. She hadn't realised just how strong that mother instinct would be, how that natural love would rush in, from the moment she'd felt Ella's first kick. The need to provide, protect, and nurture felt like an unstoppable force. It would make her strong enough to fight this battle with Alessandro...and win. She couldn't contemplate the alternative.

The limo pulled up to a tall, elegant skyscraper, and a white-gloved valet came to open her door. Mia unbuckled Ella's car seat and heaved it out, straightening her tunic top that she'd paired with loose trousers. Three months postpartum, she was still working off the baby weight, something that made her feel self-conscious when she was in Alessandro's hard, honed presence.

Inside the hotel's large and opulent lobby, all marble and crystal, a staff member met her at the door, clearly watching and waiting for her.

'Mr Costa is waiting for you in the penthouse suite,'

she informed her crisply, and Mia followed her into a glassed-in lift that soared upwards, her hands slippery on the car seat handle. She wished he hadn't asked—or, rather, commanded—that she come here, to this glamorous place, clearly his turf. It put her at a disadvantage for the battle she knew was coming, and she suspected Alessandro had arranged it for exactly that reason. Still, she would do her best to stand her ground and make her case.

The lift doors opened directly into the penthouse suite, a soaring, open space with floor-to-ceiling windows on every side. As Mia stepped out onto the white marble floor, she felt as if she were flying—or falling. The sight of the city far below all around her made her feel dizzy.

'Mia.' Alessandro's voice was a low, steady thrum as he stepped forward and took the car seat from her, smiling down at a now sleeping Ella. Mia relinquished it unthinkingly as she took a few steadying breaths to combat the sudden feeling of vertigo.

Alessandro looked devastatingly handsome, as usual, in a crisp grey suit with a cobalt-blue button-down shirt and a silver-grey tie. He smelled amazing, too, the same sandalwood aftershave that Mia remembered all too well assaulting her senses and reawakening her memories.

'Would you like a drink?' he asked politely. 'Coffee? Tea? Juice?'

'Just water, please.' On shaky legs she walked to one of the white leather sofas scattered around and sat down. 'This place is amazing.' She glanced around the huge space, noting the king-sized bed, the sunken marble tub, the glittering kitchen with top-notch appliances, all of it open plan, the different areas separated by elegant shelving and tall potted plants.

'The view sold me on it,' Alessandro said as he fetched her a glass of water. 'I wasn't sure about the open plan, but the architect insisted it was the way to go.' He handed her a glass, which Mia took with murmured thanks before sitting opposite her, one leg crossed neatly over the other as he sipped his coffee. Ella sat between them in her car seat, fast asleep.

'So,' Alessandro said, his opening gambit. 'I've arranged a flight to Rome for this evening.'

'What?' Mia nearly dropped her glass, and her surprised squawk made Ella stir in her seat before she settled back to sleep.

'Is that so surprising? I told you what I intended last night. Why should either of us linger? There's nothing for you here, Mia.'

'How would you even know that?' she demanded. She'd known Alessandro would have a plan, and even that he would insist on it, but she hadn't realised he would enact it so quickly, and without even telling her. It made her furious—and it also made her scared. He had so much more power and money than she did. His will felt like a force of nature. How could she fight it?

'You more or less admitted it yesterday,' he answered evenly. 'You've only been here for a year, and you weren't sure about coming here in the first place. Why stay?'

She'd stayed because it had been worth it financially,

and she had no job waiting for her back in London or anywhere else. What friends she'd made in London she'd lost touch with over the last year, and none of them were in a position to help her as a single mother anyway.

She'd been stuck, and Alessandro was right when he said there was nothing keeping her in California, but… that didn't mean she wanted to go to Tuscany with him.

'I'm not committed to LA, it's true,' she said carefully. 'Although I've enjoyed my job here, and I was— *am*—intending to return to it in a few months. But that doesn't mean I want to live in Italy. I don't even know the language, Alessandro.'

He shrugged, dismissive. 'You'll learn. And there's no reason for you to return to work when I will be providing for you.'

'I like working—'

'Then perhaps you can return to it when Ella is a bit older.'

Although she greatly disliked his high-handed manner, Mia wasn't willing to fight that particular battle along with all the others. The truth was, she'd rather stay with Ella when she was so little. But she still didn't want to go to Italy.

'I think we both need to compromise,' Mia said, trying not to sound desperate. 'What if I returned to London? You go there fairly often for business. You could see Ella regularly…' She trailed off at the dark look developing on Alessandro's face, like a storm front coming in, of towering black clouds.

'*That's* your compromise? I see my daughter once a month, if that?'

"FAST FIVE" READER SURVEY

Your participation entitles you to:
✳ 4 Thank-You Gifts Worth Over $20!

Complete the survey in minutes.

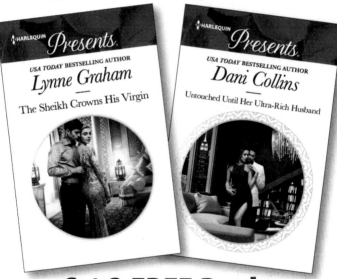

Get 2 FREE Books

See inside for details.

Dear Reader,

Since you are a lover of our books, your opinions are important to us... and so is your time.

That's why we made sure your **"FAST FIVE" READER SURVEY** can be completed in just a few minutes. Your answers to the five questions will help us remain at the forefront of women's fiction.

And, as a thank-you for participating, we'd like to send you **4 FREE THANK-YOU GIFTS!**

Enjoy your gifts with our appreciation,

Pam Powers

To get your
4 FREE THANK-YOU GIFTS:

✱ Quickly complete the "Fast Five" Reader Survey
and return the insert.

"FAST FIVE" READER SURVEY

1 Do you sometimes read a book a second or third time? ○ Yes ○ No

2 Do you often choose reading over other forms of entertainment such as television? ○ Yes ○ No

3 When you were a child, did someone regularly read aloud to you? ○ Yes ○ No

4 Do you sometimes take a book with you when you travel outside the home? ○ Yes ○ No

5 In addition to books, do you regularly read newspapers and magazines? ○ Yes ○ No

YES! I have completed the above Reader Survey. Please send me my 4 FREE GIFTS (gifts worth over $20 retail). I understand that I am under no obligation to buy anything, as explained on the back of this card.

❏ I prefer the regular-print edition
106/306 HDL GNQN

❏ I prefer the larger-print edition
176/376 HDL GNQN

FIRST NAME	LAST NAME

ADDRESS

APT.#	CITY

STATE/PROV.	ZIP/POSTAL CODE

'Surely you come to London more often than that,' Mia protested. 'To check on Dillard's...'

'Dillard's has been assimilated into Costa International, as I told you it would be. I come to London once or twice a year at most.'

And for that he'd needed to put her on the other side of the world? It was not a point Mia could afford to make now. 'But it's not that far,' she insisted, trying her best to hold on to the plan she'd come up with last night—her in London, living in familiar surroundings with some friends around, and Alessandro safely in Italy or wherever else he travelled, coming by once in a while. She could live with that. Just about.

'Not *far*?' Alessandro's eyebrows rose in incredulity before drawing together in what could only be anger. Mia tried not to shrink back in her seat. 'It's a four-hour plane ride, Mia. How often do you think I want to see my daughter? How much do you think I wanted to be involved in her life?'

She shook her head slowly, afraid to hear his answer. 'I... I don't know.'

'Then I'll tell you. Completely. I want to see her every *day*. Morning and night and even afternoon. I will not have my child growing up without a father in her life. I know what that's like and I will not allow it for Ella, especially when her father wants to be involved.'

He knew what that was like?

The terse statement made Mia realise there were depths of feeling and conviction to Alessandro's stance that she hadn't anticipated. Hadn't remotely begun to guess. 'So what exactly are you suggesting?' she asked faintly.

'You and Ella live at my villa in Tuscany. It is comfortable, in the country, the perfect place to raise a child. I will live there as well, and commute to Rome or wherever else as needed.'

'So…we'd live together?' She hadn't expected that, somehow. She'd anticipated him tucking her away, controlling her as her father had her mother. But now it almost sounded as if he expected them to play at happy families, something she really could not envision, and she doubted Alessandro had thought it through entirely.

Alessandro's frown deepened. 'Of course we'd live together.' He made it sound as if she'd asked something so obvious as to be absurd.

Mia shook her head slowly. 'That's not a given, Alessandro. I mean…we don't even know each other.'

'We have a baby together.'

'Yes, but…we're strangers.' It hurt to say it, because she'd never, ever have wanted to bring a child into the world the way she had with Ella, and yet she didn't regret her daughter for a single second.

'Then we'll get to know each other.' Again he made it all sound glaringly obvious. 'All the more reason for you to come to Tuscany, Mia.'

'So you expect me to follow you to Italy, to live in your house, without even knowing you?'

'You know enough, surely.'

'What I know I don't even like! You're ruthless, Alessandro, completely ruthless when it comes to the companies you take over—'

'That's business, and in any case, I'm not as ruth-less as you think.' He almost sounded hurt. 'I thought you realised that.'

Memories of that night flitted through her brain, the man she'd started to dream he was, as well as what she'd learned about Dillard's former employees. No, he wasn't as ruthless as all that. And yet...

'Still, you've been incredibly overbearing since you blasted back into my life,' she persisted, 'demanding everything and making no compromises—'

'Because I'm right.'

She rolled her eyes. 'Of course you are.'

'And because this is important to me.' He lowered his voice, his hands clenched together, as he struggled with a depth of emotion Mia had never seen before. 'I grew up without a father, Mia. He chose to walk away before I was born. All my life I've wondered...' He paused, cleared his throat. 'I cannot abide the thought of my daughter thinking I would do the same thing, even for a moment. I cannot countenance for a *second* that she might wonder why I don't see her more often, or why I don't live in the same country as she does. I cannot stand the prospect that she might think I don't care.'

Tears, unexpected, unwanted, crowded Mia's eyes. 'I'm sorry,' she whispered. 'I didn't realise.'

He nodded jerkily. 'Now you know.'

'But surely you can still see how much you are ask-ing of me.'

'I am asking just as much of myself. Together we will be parents for Ella. We will put aside our own desires and needs for her sake. It is what any good parent would do.'

And how on earth could she argue with that? Mia felt cornered, and yet she could hardly blame Alessandro for it. She agreed with him…she just wished she didn't. That there was another way, and yet there so clearly wasn't.

'So you want us to live together?' she surmised hesitantly. 'In the same house? What about…what about all your women?'

Alessandro looked at her as if she had sprouted horns. 'I would not have *women*.'

'At least a woman, then,' Mia clarified impatiently. 'I've seen the photos, Alessandro—'

'The only woman I will have on my arm is you,' Alessandro returned, his silver gaze snaring hers and pinning her in place. 'As my wife.'

For a second Alessandro thought Mia might faint. Her face drained of colour and she swayed where she sat, her lips bloodless as she parted them and tried to speak.

'What…?' The word was a scratchy whisper. She shook her head, looking as dazed as if she'd been hit on the head. 'What…are you talking about?'

'I thought it would be obvious.' Although he realised now what had been set in stone in his own mind had not even crossed Mia's. He'd been so sure of the way forward he might have skipped a few rather crucial steps in their conversation. Well, he would cover them now. 'I thought I'd made it clear. For Ella's sake, we will marry. You would live in Tuscany as my wife.'

'Was that a *proposal*?'

Her scathing tone caught him on the raw. He'd just offered to *marry* her, and she was acting offended. 'It was a fact,' he stated rather shortly. 'I accept that neither of us expected or even wished this, Mia, but surely we can put aside our personal preferences for Ella's sake. It's the right thing to do.'

'But you're talking about my whole life.'

'And my whole life.' He met her gaze steadily, refusing to be moved. Mia still looked as if she didn't know what had hit her.

'Alessandro, I can't marry you.'

'I'm not asking you to marry me this very minute.' He tried to ignore the sharp needling of hurt he felt at her blunt refusal. 'I understand we'll want to get to know another before we say any vows, although the sooner we make this official, the better, as far as I am concerned. Again, for Ella's sake.'

'I… I can't.' She looked agonised, strangely torn. 'Alessandro, I can't.'

'Why not?' His voice sharpened. 'Are you already married?'

'No, of course not.' She rose from the sofa, rubbing her arms as if she were cold. 'I just can't. I can't be married. I can't be married to a man like you.'

'A man like me?' His tone had turned icy. 'What is that supposed to mean?' A man of low birth? A bastard? He'd heard it all before, of course, but it still hurt coming from her.

'Just…' Mia shrugged helplessly. 'Someone so…rigid and in control. You've done nothing but order me around since I met you, Alessandro, and I can't live like that. I can't let myself live like that.'

Alessandro absorbed her words, as well as the despairing conviction behind them. 'I understand your concern,' he said finally. 'I don't want you to feel as if you've been railroaded into anything. We can leave the discussion about marriage for now. I'm not about to force you to the altar.' The very thought was distasteful. 'But I hope you can see the rightness of coming to Italy with me.'

'For ever?' Mia flung at him.

Startled, Alessandro shrugged. 'At least for an…interim period.'

'How about three months?' she challenged. 'I can just about live with that.'

'Three months,' he repeated. It wasn't so long, but hopefully long enough. 'So we can get to know one another and make sure a relationship between us will work.'

'A relationship?' She frowned. 'Are you saying that we're…*dating*?' She sounded disbelieving.

'If you are asking if there will be a physical relationship between us,' Alessandro said after a moment, feeling his way through the words, 'then I shall leave that up to you.' He could certainly give her that choice.

'You will?'

'I won't force you to the altar, and neither will I force you to my bed. You will come to it when it's your choice, not my decree.'

Colour touched her cheeks. 'So the offer's open whenever…?' she queried a bit sardonically.

'I won't deny that I still find you attractive,' Alessandro said, meeting her gaze boldly. Perhaps if she remembered just how explosive their chemistry had been, she would be less reluctant to go along with his ideas. 'What we shared was brief, I admit, but it was good, Mia. It was very good.' He held her gaze, felt his own heat, and saw that she remembered just how good it had been... just as he did.

'And what happens after three months?' Mia asked after a long, heated moment. 'If I decide it isn't working?'

Everything in him resisted such a notion, but he still made himself say the words. 'Then we will have to consider alternatives. But I hope, for Ella's sake, such a drastic step will not be necessary.'

'You call *that* a drastic step?' Mia let out a huff of humourless laughter.

'I do,' Alessandro returned evenly. 'Because it would be drastic for Ella, unable to have two loving parents in her life.' His voice rose with the strength of his emotions. He'd only held Ella once, had barely spent any time with her, but she was his and he wanted to raise her right, give her the stability and security and yes, even the love that he'd never had growing up. 'Why should I be content with seeing my daughter only on occasion, a deadbeat dad, and not by my own choosing? Why don't you want Ella to have two parents fully involved in her life, loving and taking care of her? Who doesn't want that for their child?'

'Is that...is that what it would be like?' She sounded so surprised that Alessandro felt stung.

'You don't think I would love my own child?'

'I'm not saying that, it's just…you're so focused on work, Alessandro. As far as I can tell from the tabloids, you've never had a serious relationship.'

'This is different.'

'How?'

'Because of Ella. I admit, I've never been interested in serious relationships before now.'

'And I'm still not,' Mia interjected, surprising him. 'I've never wanted to get married, be tied down—'

'Too bad you had my baby, then.'

They stared at each other, an emotional standoff, and then Mia let out a ragged sigh and sank back onto the sofa. 'I can't keep arguing about this.'

'Then be reasonable. Three months. That's all I'm asking. You wouldn't be going back to work before then anyway.'

She stared into the distance, her expression remote and a bit weary. Then, to his immense satisfaction, she slowly nodded. 'All right. Three months. I can give you that.'

'Good. We can make this work,' he said, with conviction. Mia did not reply. She stared out of the window, her expression so distant and despairing that Alessandro felt something in him shift, turn over. It was as if an emotion he'd long kept buried was stirring to life, and he didn't like it. He realised he wanted to comfort her. He didn't like seeing her sad, but he had no idea how to make her happy. Both realisations were disturbing. She'd given in to his demand and seen the sense in his plan. He should be triumphant, and instead he felt…unsettled.

'You look tired,' he said abruptly. 'Why don't you have a sleep?'

She turned to him, blinking slowly. 'A sleep…?'

'Yes, have a nap. Ella is sleeping, and I can keep an eye on her.' He gestured to the huge bed on the other side of the suite, made into its own cosy enclave with bookshelves and potted palms to give the area privacy without compromising the stunning view. 'Have a rest. You look exhausted, Mia.'

And we fly to Rome tonight.

He didn't say the words, but he had a feeling she heard them anyway.

'All right,' Mia said after a moment. 'I am very tired.'

'Good. Rest.'

He watched as she rose stiffly from the sofa, exhaustion apparent in the slump of her shoulders, the lines on her face. Compassion stirred inside him. She needed help; she needed him. He just needed to make her realise it.

Mia bent over Ella's car seat, tenderly touching her daughter's cheek before she straightened and looked straight at Alessandro.

'I don't like any of this, Alessandro, even if I recognise that our being together is best for Ella. But no matter how you spin it, I still don't feel as if I have any choice.'

'I've given you a choice,' Alessandro protested, and she nodded.

'Exactly,' she said. 'You've *given* me.' Without waiting for his reply, she turned and walked towards the bed, everything about her seeming both proud and defeated. The unsettling combination made Alessandro ache. It also made him feel guilty, as if he were doing something wrong, but he wasn't. He couldn't be.

For Ella's sake, this was how it had to be. Mia would come to accept that in time. He would make sure of it.

CHAPTER NINE

MIA STARED OUT of the window of the private jet as it lifted into the sunset sky. Her stomach clenched with nerves, her insides swooping as the plane rose and then levelled out. She was doing this. She was really doing this.

Because she had to. For Ella's sake, for Alessandro's sake. She'd recognised that this morning, when Alessandro had spoken oh-so-reasonably, but she still resisted. Still hated the thought that she was being backed into a corner.

Three months. She could manage for three months. She could get to know Alessandro. She could try to get along. After that...

Mia had no idea what happened after that.

She glanced across the teakwood table that separated her from Alessandro in the jet's sumptuous living area. Since waking up in Alessandro's penthouse that afternoon, she'd felt as if she'd fallen into a fairy tale, unsure if she was with the prince or the big bad wolf. A little bit of both, perhaps. Alessandro was certainly solicitous of her every need; she couldn't fault him even if she was still on edge.

While she'd been sleeping, something she hadn't even thought she'd be able to do, he'd arranged for all her things to be packed up from her apartment and put onto his private plane. He'd had bags packed for her and Ella with everything they could possibly need for the flight. They'd gone directly from the hotel to the airport, which meant Mia hadn't been able to say good-bye to anyone.

She hadn't made many friends in LA yet, but she still resented his high-handed manner. She didn't think he was even aware of it, which made it worse. Somehow, against everything she believed and hoped for her life, she was ending up with a man like her father. Maybe not in the needless cruelty or sneering manner—Alessandro was certainly better than that. Yet the result was the same—being controlled by a man.

Alessandro, at least, was showing himself to be an attentive father. When she'd stumbled from the sumptuous bed back in the suite, she'd found him on the sofa, cradling Ella in his lap as he cooed down at her, his face softened and suffused with love. Seeing him in that unguarded moment had given Mia the hope that maybe, just maybe, she really was doing the right thing by going to Italy. That maybe it could even be a good thing.

She glanced again at Alessandro, his profile both handsome and hard as he gazed down at his tablet, a faint frown bisecting his patrician brow. He'd shed his suit jacket and rolled up his shirtsleeves, revealing powerful forearms, muscles flexed.

Looking at him now, Mia remembered how irresistible she'd once found him. How Alessandro had informed her it was her choice whether or not she shared his bed. Her choice…and yet she was afraid to make it, afraid of feeling even more under his control, because she knew when he touched her she'd lose her sense of reason completely. And yet she couldn't get the images, the memories, out of her mind.

As if sensing her looking at him, Alessandro glanced up, his frown deepening as their gazes met. 'Is everything all right? Do you need something?'

She shook her head. She'd just fed Ella, and her daughter was asleep in her car seat. 'No, I'm all right.'

'Why don't we have champagne?' Alessandro suggested. 'To toast our future.'

'The next three months, you mean,' Mia couldn't help but correct. She needed to remind herself of that safeguard as much as him. 'I don't know. I shouldn't drink too much whilst I'm breastfeeding…'

'Surely a sip won't hurt.' Alessandro motioned to an aide, and then barked out a command in Italian. Mia watched him silently; he wasn't even aware of how once again he'd exerted his will. It was a small matter, seemingly insignificant, and yet she felt it.

She also felt how, after just one day, she was too weary and defeated to challenge him. What would she be like after a month, a year, a decade? Would she become as worn out and ghost-like as her mother had been, drifting through life, half-heartedly defending her choices, or lack of them?

The staff member came back with a bottle of champagne and two crystal flutes. Alessandro dismissed the man and then expertly opened the champagne, the cork giving a stifled pop before he poured them both glasses.

'To Ella,' he said as he handed her a glass. 'And to us.'

Dutifully Mia clinked her glass against his before taking a tiny sip. The bubbles fizzed through her, pleasantly surprising; it had been over a year since she'd had any alcohol. In fact...

'Do you remember the last time we had champagne?' Alessandro murmured, and Mia stiffened.

'I'm sure you've had champagne last week, if not sooner.'

'I haven't, but I meant when we had it together.'

Together. The word held memory as well as promise. Intent. Mia took another sip of champagne, just to steady her nerves. 'I didn't expect you to talk about that,' she said after a moment.

'Why not?'

'The last time we were *together*, you wanted to forget it, just like I did.' Her voice was unsteady, as was her hand as she put her flute of champagne on the table in front of her.

'Things have changed,' Alessandro answered with a nod towards a still sleeping Ella. 'Obviously.'

'They haven't changed that much,' Mia protested. 'You said I had three months to get to know you...to decide.' Something flickered in his face and she leaned forward. 'Did you mean that?'

'Of course.'

She scanned his taut expression, dark brows drawn

together, gaze slightly averted. 'Alessandro,' she said slowly, 'what will happen after three months?'

'My hope is we'll get married.'

'Married...' Was she a fool to think he might have relinquished that notion? 'And if I refuse?'

His eyes gleamed as he leaned forward. 'I will make it my life's mission for the next three months to make sure you don't *want* to refuse.'

His voice was a sensuous caress, yet to Mia the words felt like a threat...and one she suspected he could carry out all too well.

'And how will you do that?' she asked, her voice wobbling. She hadn't meant to direct a challenge, but she realised she had as Alessandro smiled knowingly, his lingering gaze as tangible as if he'd touched her.

'I think you know how.'

'By seducing me?'

'Do I need to remind you how explosive our chemistry was?'

'No, but perhaps I need to remind you there is more to a relationship—to a *marriage*—than what happens between the sheets.'

'Or on a desk,' Alessandro murmured, his eyes glinting.

Mia's cheeks heated and she looked away. 'Indeed.'

Alessandro settled back in his seat. 'Like I said, we have chemistry, Mia. Let's build on that.'

'That's hardly the foundation for a good marriage.' In fact she feared it could be a disastrous one. What about shared values, aspirations, ideals? And besides, she had never wanted to get married, anyway. She'd never wanted to be so in thrall to another person, so under their control…and yet here she was. It filled her with a feeling of fearful hopelessness.

'Chemistry and a shared love of a child is plenty,' Alessandro returned. 'More than many, or even most, have, and something we can build on.'

'Did your parents love each other?' she asked bluntly, and he stilled, clearly surprised by the question, before he gave a terse shake of his head.

'My mother loved my father, but he did not love her in return.'

'So would our marriage be one of love, eventually? Is that what you would hope for?'

Alessandro stilled, a guarded look coming over his face. 'Our love of Ella…'

'You know that's not what I mean.'

'What do you mean, Mia? Yesterday you told me you had never intended on marrying. Are you now telling me you want something different out of your marriage?'

She deflated, wondering why she'd pursued the point. 'No, I'm not saying that. I've never wanted to fall in love.'

'And neither have I, so I think we're a good match.'

Yet why did that make her feel so despairing, so hopeless? She'd never wanted to marry, yet now that she might, she didn't think she wanted a marriage devoid of affection. She felt trapped, choiceless, and she hated that. At least it was only for three months. It felt like the only silver lining to an otherwise towering, dark cloud.

'My parents' relationship was stormy and difficult,' Alessandro said after a moment. She had the sense he was telling her something he didn't relate often. 'They never married, and, as I told you once before, my father walked out before I was born. My mother spent the next fifteen years beaten down by life, working dead-end jobs, moving from grotty flat to grotty flat, all in pursuit of some man or other…toxic relationships with wastrels or drunks or men who only wanted one thing.' He sighed heavily, his gaze turning distant, as if he was lost or even trapped in a memory. 'And she gave her heart every time, or so it seemed to me. It was no way to live.' Mia heard a raw note of sadness in his voice that she'd never heard before, and it touched her, made her see him in a new and surprising light.

'That must have been difficult for you,' she said quietly, the aggression gone from her voice.

'It wasn't easy,' Alessandro agreed, a dark note in his voice that made Mia's heart ache. She had an image in her head of a little black-haired boy watching with wide, grey eyes as his mother invited another man into their lives, as they were forced to move, as life upended for him again and again. His childhood had been as challenging as hers, if not more so, just in a different way.

'And so this is the alternative?' she asked after a moment.

'It's *an* alternative.' Alessandro met her gaze directly, his expression now one of firm purpose. 'Give us a chance, Mia. I'm willing to. We can have a marriage of companionship and compatibility. It doesn't have to be some terrible truce, or a sorry stalemate.'

'A loveless marriage?'

'Love is overrated. You must think that yourself, with your own background. Why fall head first into something that spins out of control when you can have something so much better?'

He made it sound so reasonable. So possible. Still Mia hesitated. 'We still don't even know each other, Alessandro.'

'Which is why we're giving it three months.' He smiled and downed the rest of his champagne.

Three months, Mia thought, and then he'd expect her to marry him. And at that point, she had a terrible feeling she'd be the subject of another hostile takeover… impossible to refuse or resist. Alessandro would make sure of it.

Ella stirred in her seat, and Mia rose from where she'd been sitting. 'She needs a top-up,' she said. 'And I'm really tired. I'll feed her in bed and then go to sleep, if you don't mind.'

'All right.' Alessandro had a thoughtful look on his face as he tracked her movements. She unbuckled Ella from her seat and scooped her up, breathing in her sweet baby scent, savouring the innocence of it. All this was for Ella's sake, she told herself. Fighting Alessandro at every turn would only end up hurting Ella. For her daughter's sake, she had to get along with this man. She had to give this—them—a try, even if everything in her still railed against it.

'Please let me or a member of staff know if you need anything,' Alessandro said solicitously. 'Anything at all.'

She nodded, knowing she needed to make an effort

even though part of her resisted. 'Thank you, Alessandro,' she said stiffly.

Surprise flashed across his features, followed by a ripple of pleasure, and then he nodded. Mia turned and walked towards the back of the plane with Ella in her arms.

He should have thanked her back, Alessandro realised belatedly as Mia closed the door of the plane's bedroom behind her. She'd thanked him; he should have thanked her, for going along with his plans, for agreeing to so much. But he hadn't thought of it, and the realisation shamed him, an unexpected, unwelcome feeling.

What he was doing was reasonable and generous. He was offering Mia far more than she could ever have on her own—a lifestyle of which she would have never been able even to dream. And yet…in some way he was taking her freedom. He recognised that, just as he recognised she was taking his. Still, it had been his idea, his will. He recognised that too.

Restless, Alessandro rose from his seat to prowl the living area of the plane, knowing he wouldn't be able to work or settle to anything. He should be feeling satisfied, having arranged everything as he'd wanted it. Within twenty-four hours of arriving in California, he had Mia and his daughter back on a plane to Tuscany.

All was going according to his plan. So why did he feel so…restless? So dissatisfied and *hungry*, in a way he didn't expect or understand?

He sat down again, pulling his laptop towards him, determined to work. But after only an hour he realised he hadn't got anything done; he'd been staring at a spreadsheet of profit margins for at least twenty minutes.

With a near growl, he pushed his laptop away and strode towards the back of the plane. He could check on Mia and Ella, at least, and make sure they were okay.

He opened the door as quietly as he could; the bedroom was swathed in darkness, the shades drawn down against the night sky, the only light coming from the adjoining bathroom, the door ajar.

Mia lay on her side, her hair spread across the pillow in a golden sheet, Ella in the middle of the bed, cradled gently in her arm, both of them fast asleep. As Alessandro came closer he saw that Ella had finished feeding; a milk bubble frothed at her lips, one fist flung upwards by her round cheek. His gaze moved to Mia, and something in him jolted as he saw she'd changed into a white cotton nightgown, its buttons undone so she could feed Ella, one creamy breast on display.

All of it together—mother, child—was beautiful to him, and made him ache and yearn even more than he had before. More than he'd ever let himself.

He *wanted* this. Not just Mia, not just Ella. All of it together. *Them.* A family, the family he'd always ached for but never known. Finally, it could be his. He hadn't even realised how much he'd been missing it until it was here, offered up in front of him, tantalising and beautiful.

Resolution crystallised inside him, sharpening into focus. Whatever it took, whatever it meant, he was going to knit them into a family. He would make Mia leave her regrets and fears behind; he would work hard to make her want this as much as he did. He'd worked hard for everything in his life, he could work hard at this too, the most important thing. The most important business deal he'd ever make. Not a hostile takeover as Mia had once suggested, but a true and purposeful merger. A marriage.

Carefully, as quietly as he could, he took off his shoes and belt, leaving his clothes on for form's sake as he stretched out on the bed next to Mia, gently putting his arm around her. She stirred, and he waited, his breath held, wondering what she would do. Then she let out a breathy sigh and relaxed into him, her body softening against his.

Desire and something far, far deeper roared through him, elemental and overwhelming. Yes, he wanted this. He wanted it with every fibre of his being. And he would have it. Eventually he would have it.

Alessandro didn't know how long he slept, but he woke when Mia shifted next to him, gasping as she sat up, her hair tumbled about her shoulders, her face flushed.

'I didn't mean to fall asleep…'

Alessandro blinked the sleep from his eyes as he took in the magnificent sight of her, her body rosy and soft with sleep, her eyes bright, her nightgown still unbuttoned.

'I thought that was your intention when you lay down in bed,' he said, keeping his voice light.

'I was feeding Ella, and then I was going to put her in the Moses basket.' She nodded towards the sleeping basket that had been in her apartment, and had been brought to the plane. It was next to the bed, made up with a fleece-lined blanket.

'She can go in there now.'

'I shouldn't have fallen asleep with her on the bed,' Mia said. She sounded upset. 'It can be dangerous...'

'She's fine, Mia. Look.' With one hand on her shoulder, he turned her so they could both look at their tiny, sleeping daughter. 'She's fine. No harm done.' He rubbed her shoulder, a touch meant for comfort but which made him decidedly less so. Her skin was warm and soft, her nightgown slipping off her shoulder. He fought the urge to slip his hand inside and cup the breast he'd already seen and that was quite, quite perfect.

'Still...' Mia muttered. She sounded half-asleep.

'I'll put her in the basket now.' Awkwardly but tenderly Alessandro scooped Ella up, conscious of her fragility, her utter smallness. He still wasn't used to holding her.

The baby barely stirred as he laid her in the Moses basket, drawing the blanket over her. Then he returned to the bed, where Mia had already fallen back to sleep.

Gently he brushed a tendril of hair away from her cheek, letting his fingers skim along her silky skin. Her breath came out in a soft sigh and she relaxed against him, her body warm and pliant.

Alessandro shifted so he was lying behind her, one arm around her waist. Awareness prickled painfully through him. Sleep, he knew, would be elusive. Then Mia sighed again and wriggled closer to him, so her bottom was nestled against his groin, her head tucked under his chin. Yes, sleep would be very elusive indeed.

Alessandro kept his body relaxed so Mia would stay asleep, savouring her closeness even as it remained an exquisite form of torture. He breathed in her citrusy scent, revelling in her soft warmth, the nearness of her.

He never slept with the women he bedded. He'd always operated alone, on every level. He'd been happy with that. Yet now he found her closeness comforting, a balm as well as an undoubted enticement. He desired her, but he was also content to have her simply lie in his arms. For now, it was enough. It was more than he'd ever had before.

For a few moments he let his mind drift back over the years of his childhood, the loneliness, the uncertainty, the endless turmoil of being moved from one grotty flat to another, the parade of boyfriends who had raged or sneered or used their fists. And his mother...

But that hurt most of all. He tried never to think of his mother, to remember the look of weary defeat on her face, the words she'd said to him, too exhausted by life to be spiteful. They'd been simple truth.

'I wish I'd never had you.'

No, he didn't want to think of that. And he didn't want his daughter to wonder, even for a day, a minute, if he felt that way about her. He would love Ella the way his mother and father had never loved him. And he would build a marriage with Mia that would be better than the candyfloss froth of fairy tales, a solid relationship of affection and companionship without losing control or being vulnerable the way his mother had been. The way he'd so often felt, as a child.

And yet he recognised, as Mia slept in his arms, that he'd already lost control, in some small but elemental way. Already he'd been more open and vulnerable, more emotional, with her than he ever had with anyone before…not that she would recognise that.

He still did, and it unsettled him. He'd never told anyone about his parents, or how he'd felt as a child. Already she knew more about him than anyone else, ever.

Somehow he was going to have to find a way to have the family he wanted without losing himself in the process. He could not relinquish the solitary independence he'd cultivated since he could remember. He didn't know who he would be without it. And yet he wanted Mia and Ella in his life. He wanted the three of them to be a family.

He must have slept, because bright sunlight was visible underneath the rim of the shades as he stirred in bed, Mia wrapped even more tightly in his arms. In her sleep she'd rolled over to him, and now she was squashed up next to him so he could feel every delectable line and curve of her warm, warm body.

Her eyes fluttered open and she stared straight into his, her body stiffening as she realised how close they were.

'Good morning,' he said softly. 'Ella is still asleep.'

Mia glanced down at their nearly entwined bodies, her breasts spilling out of her nightgown, pressed up against him. Colour flooded her face as she tensed even more.

'What...?'

'You were asleep,' Alessandro said. 'So was I.'

Her cheeks were stained crimson as she scrambled out of his embrace, buttoning up her nightgown with fumbling fingers.

'I didn't...' she muttered, unable to look him in the eye.

'Nothing happened, if that's your concern,' Alessandro said equably. 'I would never take advantage of you, Mia. I promise you that.'

She opened her mouth, and Alessandro braced himself for what he was sure she would say. *You already have.* But then she closed her mouth and shook her head.

'I'm going to have a shower and get dressed before we land,' she said. 'Can you watch Ella?'

'Of course.'

She looked as if she wanted to say something more, but then she just shook her head again, slipping out of bed and hurrying to the en suite bathroom. The door closed behind her and Alessandro winced as he heard the lock turn with a decisive click.

CHAPTER TEN

Mia held Ella to her as she stepped out of the limo into the warm spring morning. Sunlight glinted off the terracotta tiles of Alessandro's villa, the Tuscan hills now covered in verdant green and bright blossom.

The place was huge and sprawling, made of white stucco, with terraced gardens on the hillside, bursting with colourful blooms. She could hardly credit that she was going to live in such a magnificent place, if just for three months.

Or maybe for ever.

Alessandro gently placed his hand on the small of her back as he guided her towards the imposing entrance. Mia's eyes felt gritty, her body aching with fatigue and jet lag despite the few hours' sleep she'd snatched on the plane, waking up so unsettlingly in Alessandro's arms. For a second, before she'd woken up completely, she'd lain there, warm and comfortable, snuggled and safe.

Happy.

She'd been completely wrong-footed when she'd realised just how much she'd cosied up to Alessandro, and meanwhile forgotten Ella entirely. He still had that devastating effect on her, she realised. Perhaps he always would—the ability to melt her insides like butter, even as he fanned her to flame. It scared her, the power he could have over her if she let him.

After they'd landed, Mia had done her best to find a cordial but formal middle ground, although he suddenly seemed intent on being close to her whenever he had the opportunity, such as now, when he gently pressed his palm to the small of her back, sending shivers of aware-ness rippling through her, before he took Ella from her.

'I'll hold her for a bit. You look shattered.'

She *was* shattered, but Ella felt like her safety shield. Without her, Mia was exposed, unsure what to do with her arms, how to look or feel. Everything about this was so incredibly strange. Whether for three months or for ever, she couldn't believe she and Ella were going to *live* here, with Alessandro, as a family.

She glanced around the soaring marble foyer in amazed disbelief. Several doors led off to various im-pressive reception rooms, and a sweeping double stair-case led to the second floor.

'This feels like a castle,' she couldn't help but say.

'And you're the princess,' Alessandro told her as he hefted Ella against his shoulder. Already he was start-ing to handle Ella with more confidence, although he still carried her as if she was so fragile she'd break… or explode.

The flashes of uncertainty Mia saw on his face as he held their daughter made her melt in an entirely differ-ent way—he could affect her heart as well as her body. Both were dangerous.

'You may do whatever you like to the place,' Alessandro continued, a look of nervousness crossing his face as Ella began to fuss. 'Redecorate however you want…it is your home, Mia. Yours and Ella's and mine. Ours.' He jiggled Ella uncertainly, and as their baby started to settle down he looked up at Mia with a small smile.

'Do you think she knows me yet?'

'She's starting to.' Ella gave Alessandro a gummy smile that made him grin back in delight.

'She smiled. She actually smiled.'

Mia couldn't help but laugh. 'So she did.' Watching Alessandro and Ella bond over something as simple as a smile made her heart ache. How could she ever contemplate ending this? Walking away from a family life that neither she nor Alessandro had ever had before?

It was just a smile, she told herself, and in any case, she didn't yet know what kind of family life they would have. How it would work. No matter what assurances Alessandro made, she wasn't yet convinced.

'Thank you,' she said. 'Where…where is my room?'

'Our room is at the top of the stairs, to the right.'

She turned to him, appalled even as a treacherous excitement made her stomach flip. '*Our* room?'

'It will be our room,' he amended somewhat reluctantly. 'For now you may have it. But I look forward to the day when we might share it.'

'If,' Mia couldn't help but say and Alessandro gave her a knowing look.

'When,' he repeated firmly. 'Definitely when. Now, why don't you go upstairs and have a bath, relax for a bit? I'll watch Ella, especially since she seems to like me now.' He smiled down at their daughter.

'She needs a feed…' Mia began, torn between wanting to rest and needing her daughter.

'I'll come and get you if she fusses.'

'You mean when,' Mia returned wryly, and Alessandro laughed.

'True enough. When.' He smiled at her, and Mia found herself smiling back. Maybe she needed to relax…not just in a bath, but with everything. With Alessandro. It was going to be a long, tense three months if she didn't.

Upstairs Mia wandered into the first room at the right, gaping at the sheer opulence of what was clearly the master bedroom. As Henry Dillard's PA, and then, briefly, Eric Foster's, she'd seen more than her fair share of luxury, even if she hadn't partaken in it directly. But this room exceeded all her expectations.

It was enormous, for a start, its tiled floor supplied with underfloor heating so Mia's feet remained toasty warm as she slipped off her shoes with a sigh of relief. A king-sized bed stood on its own dais, piled high with silk and satin pillows. A separate seating area with deep leather sofas had a stunning view of the garden below, with an infinity pool and hot tub large enough to seat twenty. Thick-pile rugs were scattered across the floor, so Mia's toes sank into their exquisite softness as she walked towards the bed.

It looked amazing, inviting, and huge. And one day—if or when—she was meant to share it with Alessandro. Why did that thought not alarm her as it should?

She couldn't deny the lick of excitement low in her belly, even as she tensed at the thought. She knew that giving herself to Alessandro again would come at an emotional cost. He might just see it as sex, but she knew she wouldn't. Already she felt herself softening to him, and it scared her. She had too many memories, too many fears, to let herself relax and trust Alessandro...even if he proved trustworthy.

She pushed such thoughts out of her mind as she turned to the bathroom, taking in the sunken marble bathtub, the shower big enough for two, the double sinks. She turned on the taps to fill the tub, and added nearly half a bottle of high-end bubble bath. She was going to have a good, long soak, and try not to think for a while, because if she did, her head might explode.

Twenty minutes later, having submerged herself in hot, soapy bubbles and nearly fallen asleep, Mia sat up suddenly as her breasts prickled and her body tensed. Faintly, so faintly, she heard Ella cry.

With a sigh she pulled the plug on the bath and swathed herself in the thick, velvet-soft terrycloth dressing gown she'd found hanging on the back of the bathroom door. She finger-combed her hair as she walked through the bedroom and then downstairs, following the sound of Ella's now shrill cries.

She wandered through several empty, elegant rooms before she spied Alessandro rocking Ella in the kitchen, a cheerful and comfortable room at the back of the house, with French windows leading out to a wide terrace with steps down to the garden.

Mia paused in the doorway, spellbound by the simple

yet heart-warming scene. Ella was crying with determination, while Alessandro danced around the kitchen, jiggling her rather desperately against his shoulder.

'Now, *bambina*, you need to settle down or you'll wake your *mamma*. Why are you upset, eh? What is there to be so sad about?' He pressed a kiss to Ella's cheek. 'Are you hungry, *cara*? Is that the problem? Am I going to have to wake your *mamma*, after all?'

'I'm already awake.'

Mia's voice came out scratchy as she absorbed the scene in front of her, let it squeeze her heart. She'd never seen Alessandro look so gentle, or approachable, or... *loving*. He'd been loving. And it gave her a glimpse of a future that didn't look as unfathomable or impossible as she'd assumed it would be. In a strange and surprising way, for a few seconds it had looked...wonderful. And that scared her too, because it was not what she'd expected, and it made her want things she was afraid to try for or even to dream about.

What if Alessandro was right, and they could have a relationship, a marriage, that was strong and true and good? Based on companionship and affection? What if that was possible?

Why did that thought both terrify and thrill her in equal measure?

Alessandro gave her an endearingly self-conscious smile. 'I guess she is hungry, as you said she would be. I've been trying to calm her, but no luck.'

'You can't provide the goods in this case,' Mia answered as she held her arms out, and Alessandro danced his way over to her, making her smile.

'Here she is.'

'Has she had a change?'

'Her nappy? Yes.'

'You changed it?' Mia couldn't keep the surprise from her voice.

'It took a few tries, I admit. Thankfully there were enough nappies. Those tapes…' He shook his head. 'They were not designed for durability. I might have to take over the company that makes them, to ensure a stronger design.'

Mia laughed at such an outrageous suggestion. 'Is that how you decide what companies to take over?'

'Actually, no.' He looked serious for a moment before he deliberately lightened his expression. 'But perhaps it will be, as far as nappies are concerned.'

'So how do you choose the companies?' she asked as she settled in a sofa in the cosy nook off the kitchen. Alessandro joined her, sitting on the sofa opposite. Conscious of his gaze on her, Mia bent her head, her damp hair falling forward as she brought Ella to her breast. When she was sure she was presentable and Ella feeding discreetly, she looked up, everything in her jolting at the sudden, blazing look in Alessandro's eyes…a look of pride and possession that made her feel a welter of unsettling sensations.

As he caught her gaze, it faded, leaving scorch marks on her soul. He gave her a small smile. 'I choose companies that have corrupt and weak leadership.'

Startled, she shook her head. 'But Henry wasn't…'

'Corrupt? No, perhaps not. But he was weak and lazy, and he was running Dillard's into the red. I estimated that in another eighteen months, none of you would have had jobs.'

'Surely not…'

He shrugged. 'Two years, at the maximum.'

'I always knew he was a bit old-fashioned,' Mia said slowly. 'And he did like his golf game…' But she'd considered those qualities endearing, rather than damaging. Now she wondered.

'As affable as he could be, he was a weak leader,' Alessandro responded firmly. 'And he would have proved disastrous for the company and its employees.'

'And you care about the employees.' Once she would have said as much incredulously, but now there was the lilt of a question in her tone. 'Because I don't understand that—your reputation is so ruthless, firing most of the employees of the companies you take over. And yet…'

Alessandro smiled wryly as he raised his eyebrows. 'And yet?'

'And yet that didn't seem to be the case with Dillard's. Most of the staff were given jobs elsewhere, better jobs by the sounds of it, and the people who were let go had very generous redundancy packages, which has to cut into your profit. But none of that seems to make it into the press.'

'No,' he agreed, sounding unbothered by that fact.

'Why? Don't you mind being portrayed as some ruthless monster?'

'No, because I can hardly be a teddy bear if I'm going to take over a company. Having a reputation helps.'

'But why do you do it?' Mia pressed. 'What are you trying to achieve?' He hesitated for a long moment, and

Mia had the sense they were on the cusp of some great and terrible revelation.

'I do it,' he finally said, 'because I cannot abide having weak or corrupt people in leadership, and I will not stand by and allow them to ruin people's lives.' He paused. 'Like my father did.'

Alessandro gazed at Mia, noticing the way her hair, like a golden slide of silk, hid her face, so he couldn't gauge her expression. He hadn't meant to make that admission, but now that he had he was glad he had. He could hardly expect Mia to come to trust him if he didn't share something of his life and past with her…even if doing so made him feel uncomfortably exposed.

'Your father?' she repeated softly. 'How…?'

'He was the CEO of a company in Rome. My mother was a cleaner in his office.' He could not keep the old bitterness from twisting his words. 'It was, as I'm sure you can imagine, a short-lived affair. He made my mother promises he never intended on keeping. And when he found out she was pregnant, he fired her.'

'Oh, Alessandro.' His name was a soft cry of distress. 'I'm so sorry.'

He shrugged one shoulder, half regretting having told her that much. It made him feel scraped raw inside, to have these old wounds on display.

'What did she do?' Mia asked softly.

'She had me, and then worked one dead-end job after another trying to make ends meet, which they rarely did. She told me about my father when I was quite small, and I followed his career, saw how he abused his power and privilege, not just with women like my mother, who had nothing, but in all sorts of ways.' He shifted where he sat, that old determination coursing through him again. 'I determined then that I would never allow people like that to abuse their power. And I've made it part of the mission of my work to take over companies that are showing such signs.'

Mia shook her head slowly. 'I had no idea…'

'You're not meant to. I can't exactly publicise what I'm doing. Hostile takeovers are just that. Hostile.'

'Still, to do something noble and never be known for it…'

The warmth in her eyes both discomfited and awed him. He realised he liked having her look at him like that, feel like that. And that was alarming.

'It's not as much as you think, Mia. Some people are still out of jobs. I have a reputation for a reason.' Why he was trying to dissuade her from thinking well of him, he had no idea. Perhaps simply because he wasn't used to it.

'Still.' She pursed her lips as she gazed down at their daughter. 'I wish I'd known earlier.'

'Well, now you know.'

Alessandro paused, watching as she cradled Ella in her arms, their daughter feeding happily, one fist reaching absently for Mia's hair.

'It occurs to me,' he said conversationally, 'that you know more about me than I know about you.'

Mia looked up, eyebrows raised in surprise. 'What do you want to know about me?'

'Everything. Anything.' He realised he was truly

curious. 'But we can start with the basics. Where are you from?'

'The Lake District.'

'A beautiful area.'

'You've been?'

He smiled. 'I've heard.'

'It is beautiful.' She looked away, seeming almost as if she was suppressing a shiver. 'Beautiful and isolated and very cold.'

'That sounds like a rather mixed description.'

She shrugged. 'I didn't like it growing up. I couldn't wait to get away.'

'Why? Just because it was cold?'

She hesitated, and he waited, sensing she had something more important to reveal. 'No, because my father was...well, suffice to say, we didn't get along.' She kept her gaze on Ella, catching their daughter's chubby hand in her own and gently removing it from her hair.

'And your mother?' Alessandro asked quietly.

'She died when I was fourteen. I'd say of a broken heart, but I know how melodramatic that sounds.'

'No.' His mother had wasted away, worn to the bone by work and poverty. It was possible, Alessandro knew, to die of things that ate at you the same way a physical disease did. 'Is your father still alive?'

'I don't actually know.' Mia looked up at him then, her blue eyes icy with a hard anger he'd never seen before, not even in their stormiest moments. 'I haven't seen him in eight years, and that is fine by me.'

'I see.' Although he didn't see the whole picture, he was starting to get a glimpse. Whatever had happened with her father, Mia clearly had emotional scars from it. He didn't know what they were exactly, but at least he knew they were there.

'Anyway.' Mia shrugged, her gaze back on Ella. 'With the background you just told me about, how did you get to be a billionaire by age—what? Thirty-something?'

'Thirty-seven. I worked my way up.'

'From slums to a billionaire lifestyle?' She shook her head slowly, seeming impressed. 'That's quite a steep climb.'

'Yes.'

'How did it happen?'

Alessandro shrugged. 'I was lucky and I worked hard. I started in property, buying rundown buildings and flipping them. It grew from there.'

'It has to have been more than luck.'

'Like I said, I worked hard.'

'Very hard, I imagine. You've always seemed… driven to me.'

'Yes, I suppose I am.' Although, coming from her, he didn't know whether it was a compliment or not.

'What about your mother?' Mia asked. 'Is she still alive?'

'Sadly, no. She died when I was nineteen, just when I was starting, but we'd lost touch a few years before.'

'That's sad.' Mia hesitated. 'It seems as if we have something in common.'

'Yes.' It saddened him, to think that both he and Mia had come from such fractured, damaged families—and it made him more determined to make sure their own little family wasn't. 'Our family doesn't have to be like that, Mia,' he said, a new note of urgency entering his voice. 'This can be a fresh start for the three of us.'

'I'd like to believe that,' she said after a moment, but her tone sounded wistful, even dubious, and that stung.

'Why can't you?'

'It's just… I don't know enough about you, Alessandro. And sometimes the past isn't so easy to overcome.'

'We're getting to know each other,' he persisted. 'And we'll keep doing that. What's your favourite colour?'

'My favourite colour?'

'We've got to start somewhere.'

She let out a little laugh. 'Green.'

'Favourite food?'

'Raspberries.'

'Favourite season?'

'Spring.' She laughed again and shook her head. 'I suppose I have to ask you all the same questions.'

'Only if you want to.'

Her mouth curved, her eyes lightening. Alessandro liked her that way. 'I do.'

'Then it's blue, steak, and autumn.'

'We're practically opposites.'

He raised his eyebrows. 'Is blue the opposite of green?'

'Maybe not. But the others…' Her laugh turned into a sigh as she glanced down at Ella, stroking her downy head. 'I don't know. Do such preferences matter, really? Shouldn't we be asking each other more important things?'

Alessandro caught his breath as he stared at her intently, trying to decipher her mood. He liked what she'd said, but she'd sounded sad. 'Such as?' he asked after a moment.

'I don't even know. Such as what you want out of life. What you value. What you believe.'

'What do you want out of life, Mia?' He spoke quietly, knowing the question was important, the answer even more so.

She looked up, her expression serious, her eyes bright. 'First, I want to keep Ella safe and healthy and happy.'

'Of course. I want that, as well. Utterly.'

'After that, I want to be independent. With my own money, my own choices. That's…very important to me.' Alessandro sensed a wealth of memory and meaning behind her words, and he nodded.

'Understandable.' He'd seen that all along, how she chafed against any autocratic commands…which, he acknowledged wryly, he had a tendency to give. But they could work on all that.

'What do you want out of life, Alessandro?' She glanced around the spacious kitchen, the sunny garden visible through the French windows. 'It seems like you have everything already.'

'I am thankful for what I have,' Alessandro allowed. 'But what I've wanted…what has driven me, as you've said…' He hesitated, feeling his way through the words. 'First, I want to protect and care for my family.'

'Yes.' The word was a soft assent.

'And second…it is similar to what you want, in a way, I suppose. I want to be in control. I don't want to have my life dictated by other people's whims or poor choices, as it was for all my childhood.'

'I can understand that.'

'Yes, it seems you can. So once again we are in accord, Mia. I think you will find we are far more compatible than you once feared.'

'Perhaps.' She didn't sound convinced, but Alessandro knew he could convince her. He had to.

'I mean it, Mia. I want this to work.'

'That's something, then,' Mia said with a small smile, and as their gazes met and tangled Alessandro found himself remembering a whole host of pleasurable things. The feel of Mia in his arms. The taste of her lips. How sleepy and warm she'd been that morning, snuggled up against him. And he thought how much he wanted to experience all of those things again, over and over.

Yet as his own blood heated, Mia's seemed to cool, for she looked away, her hair sliding in front of her face. Alessandro felt her emotional withdrawal like a physical thing.

'I should unpack,' she said as she brought Ella to her shoulder, pulling her robe closed with her other hand. 'And get dressed…'

'Your things will have been brought up to your room by the staff by now, I am sure. Alyssa and Paulo are the couple who run this place. They're very kind.'

'I look forward to meeting them.' She rose, clutching Ella to her a bit like a shield. 'Will you be…returning to Rome? For work?'

'In a few days.' Alessandro couldn't help but be stung

by the question. Did she want him gone already? Resolve hardened inside him. He would break down her defences. He would get to know her…in every possible way. 'Shall we have dinner together tonight? Alyssa is happy to sit with Ella.'

Her eyes widened and then slowly, seemingly reluctantly, she nodded. 'Very well.'

It was a grudging acceptance, and one that irked him just a little. Why was Mia so guarded? Why couldn't she enter into the spirit of what he was trying to do?

But what *was* he trying to do? Alessandro asked himself after Mia had gone upstairs and he headed to his study to check his work emails. Mia had asked him a host of serious questions that he had answered honestly, if not fully. What did he want from life? What did he want from this marriage? And how was he going to get it?

Already being with Mia was drawing emotion from him like poison from a wound. He felt it stir inside him, and it alarmed him. He did not want to be ruled by his emotions the way his mother had been, tossed on the turbulent waves of relationships that never delivered what they'd seemed to promise, and left destruction in their wake.

He'd always vowed he would never expose himself to that kind of horrible, humiliating risk. He would never need someone that way, let that need rule and ruin him. He would always stay in control—of himself, and of his emotions.

And he *could* be in control, Alessandro reminded himself. He wasn't that lost little boy, hiding in the cupboard while his mother screamed and fought with one of her many boyfriends, or curled up on a narrow bed, wondering when she'd finally come home after a night out.

He was a man in control of his destiny and his family. His relationship with—and eventual marriage to—Mia would be on his terms. And they would be favourable terms for her, undoubtedly. He would be generous, thoughtful, kind. But they would still be his.

CHAPTER ELEVEN

'AREN'T YOU HAPPY?'

Laughing, Mia tickled Ella's tummy as her daughter grinned and giggled back at her. They were sitting on a blanket in the villa's garden, enjoying the warm spring sunshine. It had been two weeks since Mia had come to Italy, and she was finally starting to relax into this strange and amazing new life of hers. She just wasn't sure whether she could trust it…or Alessandro.

He'd been a model of kindness and consideration since she'd arrived; she couldn't fault him for that. The first night he'd arranged for Alyssa to watch Ella while they'd had a candlelit supper out on the terrace, eating delicious food, drinking fine wine, and enjoying each other's company.

And Mia *had* enjoyed his company… Alessandro had kept the conversation light and sparkling, without any of the heavy issues that seemed poised to drag them down.

She'd even enjoyed the heat she'd seen in his eyes when she'd appeared, having changed into one of her few dresses that fitted her post-pregnancy figure, and when he'd taken her hand, butterflies had risen in a swarm from her stomach to flutter through her whole body and send her senses spinning.

It would be so easy, she'd reflected, to let herself fall. To forget her worries, her fears, her choices. She could just gently bob along on the overwhelming sea that was Alessandro...

And then what?

Fear had knotted in her stomach at the thought. She'd pictured her mother, looking so worn out and defeated, the wedding album open on her lap.

'He was so charming, Mia. So forceful and yet so caring. I fell for him hard... I loved him...'

No matter how many times she told herself Alessandro was not like her father, Mia knew, from both his behaviour and his admission, that he was man who liked to be in control. And that would always be a cause for alarm and even fear.

At the end of that candlelit dinner, Alessandro had brushed a gentle kiss across her lips, like a whisper of a promise.

'For now,' he'd said, and there had been so much intent in his voice that Mia had shivered. It had taken all her strength not to sway into that kiss, not to ask for more. Plead, even, and that scared her along with everything else. She wasn't ready...and she didn't know how long Alessandro would wait.

A fortnight on, Mia still slept alone and Alessandro did no more than kiss her goodnight. The kisses had become a bit more lingering, and last night Mia had found herself clutching his lapels, on her tiptoes, straining for more before she'd finally had the strength of will to wrench herself away.

Alessandro had smiled wryly as he'd cupped her cheek. 'Why are you fighting me so hard, *cara*?' he'd asked gently.

Because I don't know what else to do. How to be. I'm afraid of giving you everything and you taking it. What will happen to me then?

Mia hadn't had the courage to say any of it, and so she'd just shaken her head and backed away, her body trembling from Alessandro's touch. And he'd let her go, but they'd both known, if he'd wanted to, he could have made her stay.

'Hello to my two gorgeous girls.' Smiling, Alessandro strolled across the lawn to meet them, dropping a kiss on Mia's head before sitting down next to her and tickling Ella's tummy just as she had done. 'She seems happy.'

'Yes, she's very smiley this afternoon.' Mia glanced at him, feeling shy and overwhelmed as she so often did when in his magnetic, compelling presence. He was dressed casually in dark trousers and a grey polo shirt that brought out the silver in his eyes, his hair gleaming blue-black and ruffled by the warm breeze. The sandalwood scent of him still made her senses reel. 'Have you finished your work already?'

'Yes, but I need to go to Rome tomorrow morning, for a few business meetings, as well as a charity ball in the evening.' Alessandro had been working remotely from the villa, with just a few trips to various cities across Europe. Mia wondered how long he could keep such a pattern; he was a very busy, powerful man, with many demands on his time. Surely this idyll couldn't last…and part of her craved a relief from the tension of being with him, even as another part knew she would miss him.

'I think we'll manage to keep ourselves busy,' she said. Over the last few weeks she'd had a few forays into the market town for trips to the shops, and also a baby group that met in a community hall. She was also hoping to start learning Italian, although Mia was wary of putting down too many roots. This still felt temporary rather than like real life, although perhaps that would change the more effort she made.

'Actually,' Alessandro said after a moment, 'I was hoping you would come with me.'

'With you?' Mia was startled. 'But won't Ella and I just be in your way?'

'Not Ella, just you.' His gaze was warm as it met hers and lingered there with intent. 'Just for the evening, so we can spend some time together. Alyssa can watch Ella.'

'You want me to go to a *ball*?'

'Why do you sound sceptical? We've been to one before.'

'I know, but…' Mia felt her cheeks flush as she remembered the last ball they'd been to…and what had happened afterwards. 'I don't have anything to wear.'

'That's easily remedied. I can have a stylist come with a selection of gowns.'

'As you did before?'

He shrugged. 'It's not a problem.'

But it felt like a problem, because Mia wasn't sure she was ready for a night out with Alessandro. Her already wavering defences might crumble completely… and then what?

It was the question that always rose to the front of her mind, popping like a bubble before she could answer it. If she stopped trying to protect herself, keep a safe distance, what would happen?

'What are you scared of, Mia?' Alessandro asked. 'It's just a ball.'

'I know, but…'

'We'll be home before midnight, I promise. And Alyssa will enjoy taking care of Ella.'

'It's not that.'

'Then what?'

He sounded so patient, even tender. How could she doubt him? How could she be so afraid? Mia knew she wasn't being fair, holding back the way she was. Alessandro had been more than generous, more than patient with her. She needed to give something back.

'All right,' she said at last. 'I'll come.'

'Good.' He leaned forward to brush her lips with his, making her whole body tingle. 'I look forward to it. I'll arrange for the stylist now.'

As he left to make the call, Mia realised that, despite her reservations, she wanted to go. She wanted to dress up and walk into a ballroom on Alessandro's arm, just as she had once before. She wanted to spend the evening—and maybe even the whole night—with him. Saying yes had freed her to admit to herself just how much she wanted him, despite her fear. It felt dizzyingly wonderful…as well as incredibly terrifying.

'Here we are.'

Alessandro followed the bellboy into the penthouse suite of the luxury hotel by Rome's Spanish Steps, Mia walking slowly behind them. Since leaving the villa— and Ella—she'd been quiet, even subdued, perhaps wary. Alessandro knew she didn't trust him yet, but at least she'd agreed to come tonight. He hoped to prise her even more out of her shell tonight.

He'd spent the last two weeks trying to gain her trust, win her confidence, and slowly, ever so slowly, he'd felt Mia soften towards him, and he wanted to see—and feel—that even more tonight.

'Wow.' Mia stood in the centre of the large, luxurious living room, with French windows leading out to a wide terrace that overlooked the Spanish Steps. A platter of fresh fruit had been placed on a coffee table, along with bottles of champagne and sparkling apple juice. 'But we're not even staying the night…'

'I own this hotel, and the penthouse is reserved for my exclusive use. I like to have a base while in Rome.' He checked his phone. 'The stylist will be here with a selection of gowns shortly.'

'Will you need final approval, like you did before?' she said, her voice teasing. Alessandro smiled, glad for the bit of banter.

'I think I can leave that to you this time. I look forward to being surprised.'

'All right.' Mia glanced around the living room

again, taking in the silk-striped sofas, the original artwork, the marble-topped tables. 'This place really is amazing.'

'I just want you to enjoy everything, Mia,' Alessandro said. 'This evening away is meant to be a break for you, although I know you're worried about leaving Ella.'

'I know it is.' Mia rubbed her arms as if she were cold and then walked to the French windows, before opening them and stepping out onto the terrace. After a second's pause Alessandro followed her, breathing in the balmy air as he joined her at the railing overlooking the city far below.

'What's wrong?' he asked quietly. 'This isn't just about leaving Ella for a few hours.'

'No.' She shook her head. 'It's about…about us.' She glanced at him, her face troubled. 'You've been wonderful these last few weeks, I know. I can admit that.'

'Admit it?' Alessandro tried to keep his voice light, even though he was a bit stung by her words, the reluctance of them. 'You almost sound as if you don't want to.'

'I don't,' Mia admitted. 'It's just… I'm scared, Alessandro. I told you I never wanted to marry or give my life over to another person. A man. And yet here I am.'

'Yes, but…' Alessandro had to feel his way through the words. 'It doesn't have to be something to resist, Mia. We were both in agreement, I thought, about what our relationship could look like. Companionship, trust, affection.'

'And not love.' She spoke flatly, making him hesitate.

'Have you changed your mind on that?'

'No.' She sounded disconcertingly firm. 'It's just difficult to trust you.'

'Have I ever done anything to make you distrust me?' he asked, stung again by her honest admission. What had he done to make her so wary?

'Not recently.'

'What is that supposed to mean?'

'You spend your life taking over other people's businesses,' she said after a moment. 'And sometimes that feels like what you're doing with me.'

Disconcerted, Alessandro did not reply for a moment. Yes, in his own mind he had compared his relationship to Mia in terms of a takeover, although perhaps a merger was a better way of putting it, but it wasn't *hostile*. At least, it didn't have to be.

'I thought you'd agreed this was best for Ella. And I thought you'd enjoyed the last few weeks.' He couldn't keep an edge of affront from entering his voice. It was hardly as if he'd kept her in prison. 'Please believe me, Mia, I am not trying to force you into anything.'

'There are more ways to force someone than strong-arm them.'

'What are you trying to say?'

'I don't *know*,' Mia said helplessly. 'Like I said, I'm scared, Alessandro. You can be ruthless. I know you like to be in control. I understand why you do, but those things scare me.'

'I am hardly going to be ruthless with my family.'

'How do you even know that? You've kept yourself from relationships for so long. Do you even know how to be in a family relationship, one that isn't driven by anger or revenge?'

Hurt flashed through him at her words. 'I can try,' he said quietly, and her face crumpled a little bit.

'Do you really want to?'

'Of course I do,' he snapped, but he heard the anger in his voice and he knew it was wrong. He just didn't know how to show her how he felt. How much he felt. 'I know I like to be in control. But I'm not dictating things to you, Mia. I'm trying to have a real relationship with you, even if I don't understand yet all that it means.' He felt far too vulnerable having admitted that much, and so he pressed his lips together and stayed silent.

'I'm sorry.' She smiled sadly. 'And I need to try, too. I'm sorry I'm so reluctant. It's just…' She paused, and he waited, sensing she was going to say something more. But then she sighed and shook her head. 'I'd better go and choose my dress.' Her lips twisted wryly. 'That's at least one choice I can make.'

The stylist arrived a short while later, and Alessandro busied himself with work while the stylist and her assistants commandeered the bedroom for their beautifying purposes.

As he half listened to the sound of the women chatting in the next room, he found he could not focus on the work in front of him. He kept going over his conversation with Mia in his mind, as if testing it for weaknesses. Why was Mia so wary with him still? What more could he do to gain her trust? He felt as if she questioned his every motive, which made him question them, as well. Was he doing the right thing?

Of course he was. For Ella's sake as well as theirs. He just needed to be more patient. Perhaps Mia just needed more time.

Still, he couldn't keep from feeling a flicker of irritation along with hurt. He'd been trying so hard for the last few weeks, and he'd given Mia everything. What possible cause could she really have to complain? So he liked to be in control. That was hardly the worst thing, was it? It wasn't as if he was abusing his position of power, or forcing her to do something against her will.

Her reluctance annoyed him, but it also made him even more determined. He would win her yet. Whatever aspect of their inevitable relationship Mia was resisting, Alessandro would discover it and deal with it.

Which, he realised uncomfortably, *did* make this all seem a bit like the takeover she'd suggested. But it wasn't, not like that. It was just…strategy. Common sense.

He slid his hand into the pocket of his jacket, his fingers curling around the small black velvet box. Nothing, he told himself. Mia would find fault with nothing. He'd make sure of it.

An hour later, Alessandro had changed into a tuxedo and was waiting for Mia in the living room of the suite, trying to curb his impatience. It felt as if she'd been in the bedroom for ages, and he'd heard the chatter and giggles drift out as he'd wondered just how long it took to find a dress.

'She's ready,' the stylist, Elena, sang out as she came into the living room, followed by her bevy of assistants. 'And she's perfect.' She simpered at Alessandro before she thankfully excused herself, her assistants following, so Alessandro and Mia would be alone. He would be sent the undoubtedly outrageous bill later.

'Mia...?' Alessandro called when she still hadn't come out after Elena had left. 'Are you coming?'

'Yes. Sorry.' With a nervous little laugh, she stepped out of the bedroom. Alessandro sucked in his breath. He'd already seen her in an evening gown, a year ago, when he'd lost his head over the slender woman dancing in his arms.

Tonight he felt himself lose everything else. His mind emptied and his heart tumbled in his chest as Mia smiled uncertainly. 'Do you...do you like it?'

'I love it,' he assured her huskily. The gown was a pale, creamy ivory, with a delicate overlay of gold lace. Strapless, with a full skirt, it reminded him of a wedding dress, and that seemed appropriate indeed. 'Your hair...' he murmured, coming forward to loop one golden curl around his finger.

'She curled it,' Mia said nervously. 'I've never had curly hair before.'

'It's gorgeous.' Half being pinned up, the other half tumbled over her shoulders in glossy, golden waves and curls. Gently, his finger still twined in her hair, Alessandro tugged her towards him. Mia came, a smile trembling on her lips.

'Alessandro...'

'You're so beautiful, Mia. Even more beautiful now that you're a mother.'

'No...' She let out an uncertain laugh. 'I haven't lost all of my baby weight...'

'I don't want you to. You're perfect just as you are.'
He knew it sounded like well-worn flattery, but the truth
was he meant every word. He wasn't saying it to please
her or to get what he wanted, as she so often seemed
to suspect, but because he *needed* to. Because it was
right, and it was the truth.

Which was why he had to kiss her, as well.

'Mia…' Her name was a question and as she moved
closer, her silence was his answer. He placed one hand
on her bare shoulder, her skin cool and soft beneath his
palm. Then he brushed his lips across hers, softly first,
another question.

And she answered again with silence, her mouth
opening under his, a thousand times yes. Here was another truth, in the simple purity of their kiss, their lips
joining together in a brief moment that spun on and on
as Alessandro deepened the kiss, unable to keep himself
from it, losing himself in her soft and willing response.

Mia clutched his shoulders as she anchored herself to
him, to their kiss, and the world seemed to spin around
them. It was just a kiss, and yet so much more. It felt
like a promise as well as a seal.

Finally Alessandro lifted his head, breathing rag-
gedly, dazed by the intensity of the moment. Mia
blinked back at him, her fingers at her lips. Neither of
them spoke.

Alessandro felt the weight of the black velvet box in
his pocket, and he almost reached for it. Now was the
perfect moment—and yet perhaps too perfect. The last
thing he wanted was for Mia to think he was orchestrat-

ing the moment when in truth he'd been felled by it… as she seemed to have been.

So instead he left it where it was, and smiled at her instead. And, needing no words, he took her by the hand and led her from the room, out into the warm, spring night and the promise it surely held.

CHAPTER TWELVE

MIA'S HEAD WAS SPINNING. Her lips were buzzing. And as she and Alessandro moved through the party, meeting and chatting to people, she wondered if she was falling yet again for the fairy tale. Just as before, she was Cinderella for a night, and yet so much more was at stake. Her whole life. Ella's life. Their future together. It all felt as if it hung in the balance now; all she needed to do was say yes.

And for once, with the memory of Alessandro's kiss on her lips, she didn't want to wonder or doubt. She wanted to enjoy the fairy tale; she wanted, at least for tonight, to trust Alessandro's tempting promises. To believe in them and let them sweep her along.

For once she wanted to resist not only Alessandro, but also her own negative history, her persistent belief and fear that keeping herself apart from Alessandro was the only way to stay strong. To feel independent. What if staying strong could mean something else? It could mean choosing him, rather than fighting him. Was it possible?

She pressed her fingers to her lips as she recalled yet

again that heart-stopping, breath-stealing kiss. Alessandro had seemed as affected as she'd been. For a few moments, they'd shared something wonderful.

But was it—could it be—real?

Dared she let it be real in her own mind, never mind Alessandro's?

Her thoughts tumbled and shifted in her mind in an ever-changing kaleidoscope that she struggled to make sense of. She felt as if she were teetering on a precipice, but she had no idea what lay ahead—or below.

Then Alessandro took her hand as he drew her towards him, his eyes the colour of smoke, his voice husky as he devoured her in a single glance.

'Dance?'

Mia thought of their dance a year ago, when everything had heightened and changed between them. It had been magical…but it had also been dangerous. Where was the danger now? Was it real—or was she imagining it, because she was so afraid of losing herself the way her mother had? Could she let go of it for a night?

Could she let go of it for ever?

She nodded, her palm sliding across his, fingers twining and tightening as they moved onto the dance floor and began to sway to the sensuous music.

'Are you enjoying tonight?' Alessandro asked as he moved her slowly and languorously around the floor, their hips bumping, heat flaring.

'Yes…'

'You don't sound entirely convinced.' He spoke lightly but Mia saw the flash of concern and even hurt in his eyes, quickly masked.

'I don't know what to think, Alessandro,' she confessed quietly. 'So I'm trying not to think at all. I just want to…feel.'

'Feeling is good,' Alessandro murmured huskily. 'Feeling is very good.' His forehead crinkled in a frown. 'But you don't need to be so wary, Mia. So scared.'

'I'm trying not to be.'

'What exactly is it you are afraid of, *cara*?' The endearment slipped easily from his tongue, caressing her with its intimacy, making her want even more to trust this and believe in it. In him.'

She hesitated, unsure what to say. How much to confess. Yet surely Alessandro deserved to know why she was the way she was, what experiences had formed and shaped her, and that she was becoming desperate to shed now? 'I'm scared of losing myself,' she admitted quietly.

Alessandro's frown deepened, a deep line bisecting his brow. 'Losing yourself?'

'Yes. Losing my…my sense of self, I suppose. My ability to make decisions, to be my own person…' She trailed off, realising how vague and really rather ridiculous she sounded. What did it even mean, to lose yourself? Could she even put what she was so frightened of into concrete ideas and absolutes? Or was it just this vague sense of dread, that life was spinning out of control, that she needed to leave behind her, finally and for ever?

'I don't understand,' Alessandro said as he moved her around the dance floor, one hand warm and sure on her waist. 'Please, will you explain it to me?'

She shook her head. 'I don't know if I can. I know it sounds silly and vague, formless, but…it's what I grew up with. My mother and father…' She faltered, her throat growing tight with memories.

'Your mother and father?' Alessandro prompted gently. 'You mentioned you didn't get along with your father…'

'No, I didn't. He was…very controlling. Mostly of my mother but, after she died, also of me.' She shook her head, unwilling to explain just how cruel her father could be, how domineering. She didn't want to explain about the memories that still tormented her—when he'd locked her in her room, or thrown the meal her mother had made in the bin, claiming it was inedible.

He's just got high standards, Mia. That's all it is.

She couldn't explain the choking frustration she'd felt with her mother, and then later the awful fear she'd felt for herself, knowing she had to get away before her father controlled her completely.

'Controlling,' Alessandro repeated in a neutral voice. 'This is why you have this issue with control? Why you feel I am too controlling?'

'Yes,' she whispered. 'I suppose so. My father was… awful. He told me what I had to do, or say, or even wear. He enjoyed exerting that power, simply because he could.'

'And so you think I am like this man?' Alessandro asked. His voice was even, but Mia felt the hurt emanating from him, and a wave of sorrow and regret rushed through her.

Alessandro was *nothing* like her father. The realisation washed through her in a cleansing flood. Yes, he could be brutal in business, ruthless in his ambition, but he was never cruel. He'd already shown her how his hostile takeovers were, in essence, mercy missions. Although he could be autocratic, he never sneered or insulted or mocked simply to show his power, because he could. His kindness was genuine.

'No,' Mia said quietly. 'I don't think you're like him, Alessandro.' Another realisation was jolting through her, more powerful than the first. No, she didn't think Alessandro was like her father, not really. Not at all.

But maybe she was like her mother.

That, Mia realised, had been her real fear all along. Not that she'd be beholden to a man like her father, but that she would act like her mother. She wouldn't be able to help herself. She'd fall in love with Alessandro, just as her mother had with her father, and give up everything for him—willingly. *That* was what she was afraid of.

Yet how could she admit so much to him now? The last thing she wanted Alessandro to know was the hold he had over her, or that even now she was halfway to falling in love with him, and fighting it all the way.

'I understand why you would be wary, Mia,' Alessandro said. 'Of course I do. But if you know I am not like that…'

Mia shook her head helplessly. The problem was her—her weakness, and her fear. Yet did loving someone have to mean losing yourself? If Alessandro wasn't like her father, was there really any danger? Did she want to be so in thrall to her past and her own fears that she missed out on life, on love?

Yet Alessandro had never said anything about love.

'Mia?' Alessandro prompted gently. 'What is going on inside that beautiful head of yours? Tell me, so I can help.'

'I don't know,' she confessed. 'A million things. I've always believed I would never get married. I'd never...' She hesitated, for she'd been about to say love, and she wasn't ready for that. She was quite sure Alessandro wasn't, either. 'I'd never have that kind of relationship,' she amended. 'And I never wanted it. But now...'

'Now?'

'Now we have to have some kind of relationship, and yes, it scares me. But part of me...wants it, and that scares me, too.'

'All this fear.' The music had ended, and Alessandro stopped their swaying, raising her hand to his lips. He brushed a kiss across her knuckles as his gentle yet determined gaze met hers. 'I will do my best to allay your fears, *cara*. The last thing I want is for you to be afraid—of me, of anyone or anything. I promise never to hurt you, never to take advantage of you, never to make you regret joining your life with mine.'

'Those are big promises, Alessandro,' she whispered shakily. Yet she knew he meant them.

'Yes, they are.' Her hand was still at his lips as he kept his gaze on her, now fierce and glittering. 'Do you believe me, Mia? Will you trust me?'

Could she?

'I want to,' she whispered.

'Then let yourself. See what can be between us, Mia. Discover how good—how wonderful—it could be, if you let yourself trust. *Fall.* I'll catch you. I promise I will.'

His words were a siren song that she ached to listen to, and believe. If only it could be so easy. If only she could leave her fears behind and step into this bright, glittering future Alessandro promised. *Why not?* Why not at least try, for Ella's sake, for her sake, for *theirs*?

'All right,' she whispered, and Alessandro smiled, victory lighting his eyes as he drew her towards him and kissed her right there on the dance floor, in front of the crowd, his lips on hers like a seal, branding her with his mouth just as he had with his words.

As they broke apart, Mia's lips buzzed and her face flamed. She felt as if she'd just jumped off a cliff, and she couldn't yet tell whether she was flying—or falling.

'Shall we go?' Alessandro murmured, and she knew what he was asking. They'd been on a dance floor before, in thrall to their shared desire, and he'd asked her the same question. And once again, she could agree, she could let herself be caught up in what was spinning out between them, let it sweep her along so she didn't have to think or wonder—or fear.

'Yes, let's,' she whispered, and Alessandro laced his fingers through hers once more as he led her through the crowd, the faceless blur barely registering as they left the ballroom and, just as they had once before, stepped out into the warm spring night.

They were both quiet during the limo ride to the private airport where they took a helicopter back to the villa. Mia's heart thudded in her chest as she thought about what was ahead of them, what she'd agreed to.

No regrets…

The short helicopter ride seemed over in a moment, and then they were walking up towards the darkened villa, Mia achingly aware of Alessandro's powerful body next to hers. With murmured thanks, he dismissed Alyssa, who assured Mia that Ella had gone to sleep with no problems, and was still sleeping soundly.

At the bottom of the sweeping staircase, Mia paused as Alessandro stood there, his eyes blazing silver as he looked at her, the villa dark and silent all around them.

What was he waiting for?

Why wasn't he taking her in his arms, kissing away the last of her fears and objections? She was ready to be swept up in something bigger than herself, ready to let herself go. At least she hoped she was.

'What now?' she finally asked, when she could bear the silence no longer.

Alessandro met her gaze directly, his hands spread wide. 'You tell me.'

She eyed him uncertainly. 'What do you mean?'

'This moment is yours, Mia. You choose it. You decide what you want now, how far you want this to go.' He drew a shuddering breath. 'Do you want me?' Although his voice was assured, the question held a stark note of painful vulnerability that touched Mia deeply.

For the first time Alessandro was surrendering his control…and in this, the most important and elemental aspect of their relationship.

She'd been fully anticipating him to sweep her into

a masterminded and smoothly thought out seduction, and she'd been willing to go along with it, to be caught up in it and, in a way, relieved of any real and active choice…even though that was what she'd been fighting for all along.

But Alessandro wasn't giving her that option. He was making her choose now, making her fully own the decision she thought she'd already made, back in the ballroom. This could be no silent surrender, defeat by acquiescence, overwhelmed by his sheer force of personality and innate authority that she tried to resent and yet somehow craved. Alessandro wouldn't let it be that. He was making this moment hers, making her choose it to be theirs.

He held her gaze, his eyes burning fiercely, his hands still spread open wide, his stance one of acceptance rather than aggression or authority. For once he was giving her all the power, all the control, all she'd said she wanted…so what was she going to do?

Alessandro waited, his body tense, his heart thudding. Everything in him resisted this moment, the utter, revealing weakness of it. He didn't do this. He didn't let someone else choose his fate, even if just for a night, although this was so much more than a night. He'd always, *always* been the architect of his own ambition.

But over the course of the evening, as he'd reflected on what Mia had shared about her family and her past, he'd realised that in this, of all things, she needed to have the control. He needed to surrender it, even if everything in him still fought against it. And so he waited.

Mia stared at him for a long moment, a thousand emotions chasing across her lovely face, making her eyes sparkle and her lips tremble. 'Do I want you?' she repeated slowly, her voice sliding over the syllables, testing them out, and Alessandro tensed even more, waiting, expectant. *Afraid.*

Then, to his deep disappointment and dread, she shook her head. 'Not like that,' she said, with a nod towards the bedroom waiting upstairs, with its sumptuous king-sized bed and all that it beckoned and promised. The sour taste of rejection flooded his mouth, overwhelmed his senses with the unwelcome acid of it.

She didn't want him.

'At least, not *just* that,' Mia clarified, her voice trembling. 'I don't want another night with you, Alessandro, amazing as the last one was, with all of its repercussions.'

She smiled wryly, straightening her shoulders, and Alessandro raised his eyebrows, his stomach clenched hard with anxiety and uncertainty, both which he hated feeling. He'd never felt so vulnerable, so needy, so open to hurt and pain. 'What, then?' he demanded in a raw voice.

'I came up here prepared to be…to be swept away,' she began haltingly. 'I was expecting you to do the sweeping. Then I wouldn't have had to think or wonder or doubt. I could just let myself feel.'

Which sounded pretty good to Alessandro in this moment. Had he made a mistake, in surrendering his own agency? He had been taking a risk, but it was one he had hoped would turn in his favour. Now he wasn't so sure.

'And now?' he made himself ask, although he half dreaded the answer.

'And now I want something else. Something more.'

'More…'

'I don't want a night. I want…' She swallowed, more of a gulp, her eyes huge in her face as she looked at him resolutely, her chin tilted upwards in determination, her slender body trembling with emotion. 'I want for ever.'

Surprise and a far greater relief rippled through him. She wasn't rejecting him. *Them*. 'For ever…'

Her smile trembled on her lips. 'I know you've been hoping or even expecting me to marry you. But I want this to be on my terms, and amazingly you seem to want that, too. So now I'm the one proposing. The one choosing. Will you…will you marry me?'

He laughed, the sound one of shock but also admiration. He hadn't expected *that*. 'You know I will. In fact…' Fumbling a little, he reached for the small box of black velvet that had nestled in his pocket all evening. 'I was planning to make you a proper proposal tonight, but I didn't want to seem as if I was pressuring you, or arranging things somehow…' He held the box out in the palm of his hand. 'But I can't think of a better moment than this one.'

'Nor can I.' Smiling a little, she reached for it. Alessandro held his breath as she carefully opened the box, her eyes widening at the sight of the simple solitaire diamond nestled amidst its soft velvet folds. 'It's beautiful, Alessandro.'

The ring was stark in its simplicity, a single diamond on a band of white gold. Alessandro had looked at various rings, but they'd all seemed fussy and officious rather than the simple, pure statement of his intent he wanted. *Their* intent, for a life lived together. Mia lifted her face so her eyes, now luminous with the sheen of tears, met his once more. 'Will you put it on me?'

'Of course.' His fingers trembled a little as he took the ring from the box and slid it on her finger, where it winked and sparkled, a promise they were making to each other. He clasped her hand with his own. 'Do you mean this, Mia?'

'Yes.'

'You want this?' he pressed, because somewhere along the way that had become important, too. This wasn't just about winning any more, or getting what he wanted. He needed her to want it, as well. To want *him*.

'Yes.' Her voice quavered. 'I'm scared, Alessandro. I can admit that. I don't know what the future holds, but I also know I don't want to be enslaved to my past. So yes, I want this. For Ella's sake, and perhaps even for…for ours.' Her worried gaze searched his face as she nibbled her lip. 'I know we haven't actually talked about what a marriage between us would look like, besides the obvious…'

No, they hadn't. For a moment Alessandro couldn't speak, as realisation caught up with him and he desperately tried to order his jumbled thoughts. He'd been so focused on Ella, on their being a family, that he hadn't completely considered what their relationship—their *marriage*—would actually look like. What it would mean.

And he was conscious, incredibly so, that in accepting his proposal, or, rather, offering her own, Mia was giving herself to him. Her body, her mind, and yes, perhaps even her heart. Her life. Precious, fragile gifts. And he was even more conscious that in offering them, she'd, inadvertently or not, given him back the power she hated to relinquish, and which he'd always craved.

What if he hurt her?

What if she hurt him?

The second question, he told himself, wasn't a consideration; he would not allow that to happen. He would honour his marriage vows, and give Mia respect and companionship and so much pleasure. Of that he was sure. But as for love? His heart? The ability to reach inside and hurt him?

No. He saw where that led. He'd seen and felt the pain and brokenness all through his childhood. His mother's tears, anger, addictions, helplessness and grief. No. He could not offer Mia that kind of love.

But what he could offer…he'd make sure she'd be happy with. She'd want for nothing. He'd treat her like a queen.

'We'll figure it out as we go along,' Alessandro told her, smiling to soften the prevarication of his words, and what they both knew he wasn't saying. Wasn't promising. He saw it in the cloudy flicker of her eyes, the slight downturn of her mouth before she made herself smile back. 'This is going to work, Mia. I will do my best, my utmost, to give you everything. To never hurt you.' Again he felt the weight of what he wasn't saying.

To love you.

She nodded slowly. 'I know you will, Alessandro.'

'When shall we marry?'

'There's no real rush, is there?'

'Why not make it official?'

'We still could use the time to get to know each other,' Mia protested. 'The three months…'

'It's already been nearly three weeks,' Alessandro returned. Why not marry sooner?'

'At least give it a couple of weeks, so we can plan.'

'Very well.' He could wait that long. 'Are there people you want to invite?'

She shook her head. 'No, not really.'

'Then it will be just us, and Ella, exactly as it should be.' He smiled, liking the thought. 'A family from the beginning.'

'Yes.' She smiled back, but he saw a tiny frown puckering the ivory smoothness of her brow, and he drew her towards him for a lingering kiss. 'We will do this properly, and wait for our wedding night,' he said, savouring the thought. 'Trust me, Mia, our marriage will be the beginning of everything.'

CHAPTER THIRTEEN

SHE WAS A married woman.

Mia gazed down at the two rings now sparkling on her finger, the first the elegant solitaire diamond from the night of her proposal, the second a simple band of white gold that Alessandro had slipped on her finger only moments ago.

They were standing on the terrace at the villa in Tuscany, the gardens and hills spread out before them in all their blossoming glory, the sun shining benevolently down. Alyssa and Paulo had been the witnesses to their wedding, the local priest, a smiling man who spoke no English, the officiant. Ella, clasped in Alyssa's arms and gurgling happily, had been the only guest.

Mia had worn a strapless dress of ivory silk that she'd bought in Rome on an extravagant shopping trip last week; Alessandro had insisted she buy a complete trousseau, including some very sexy lingerie that made her heart race just to look at.

The last three weeks had been a whirlwind, and a wonderful one at that. Mia had let her fears trickle away in the blazing certainty of Alessandro's attention. He doted on Ella and was kind and considerate with her, and the kisses that punctuated each evening had become longer and more lingering, leaving Mia in a welter of unsated desire, wondering why Alessandro insisted they wait, even as she acknowledged she was glad that he had.

He'd given her no reason to doubt the sudden, surprising choice she'd made that night after the ball, when she'd turned down the offer of a night for so much more.

Mia had been shocked by her own audacity and conviction, but in that moment she'd felt the rightness of what she was doing...what *they* were doing.

She could trust Alessandro. That, she realised, was the choice she was making.

With the ceremony finished, Alyssa handed Ella to Paulo, who took the baby with smiling ease, as she went to fetch the refreshments. Alessandro came to stand by Mia, placing a hand on her lower back, warm and sure, as he smiled down at her.

'Happy?' he murmured, and she turned to smile at him, realising that she really was. Over the last few weeks, her fears and doubts had been chipped away until there was very little of them left.

The dread that had taken residence in the pit of her stomach like some fermenting acid no longer pooled there. Yes, she was still afraid, but it was the uncertain nervousness of a new bride rather than the consuming fear of a woman on the brink of some awful abyss.

She *was* on the brink...but perhaps of something wonderful. Mia was trying to stay pragmatic, reminding herself that Alessandro had made no declarations of love, and neither had she. They didn't know each other well enough for that yet, and she still wasn't entirely sure she wanted to give him that much of herself.

And yet, despite her reservations, the possibility remained, in her heart at least, that this could be a marriage not just of convenience and companionship, which Alessandro had already promised, but also of love, something he most certainly had not. Something she'd never let herself consider before, but was now allowing herself to cautiously wonder about, if just a little.

'Yes, I'm happy.' She gazed out at the gardens, burgeoning with blossom and scent. 'It's been a perfect day.'

'You didn't mind not having a big wedding?'

Mia shook her head. 'I never intended on getting married at all, so why would I want a big wedding?' she answered with a little laugh. She glanced again at the rings on her finger, a tremor of excitement rippling through her at the sight of them. There was no going back.

She might have never thought she'd marry, and yet here she was. Here they were…and tonight would be their wedding night. Already nerves sizzled through her at the thought of that.

'Most young girls dream of big, white weddings,' Alessandro remarked.

'Not me. This has been perfect, truly.' She rested one hand on his, curled around the balustrade, the sun warming their skin. 'I couldn't ask for anything more, Alessandro.'

'Nor could I.' He smiled at her, his expression warm

and glinting, allaying the last of her fears. This was going to work. It already was working. Then Alessandro nodded towards Alyssa, who was bringing out a magnificent *millefoglie*, the traditional Italian wedding cake of puff pastry, Chantilly cream, icing sugar and strawberries. 'Shall we have cake?'

'I can always have cake.' Mia took Ella from Paulo as Alyssa cut the cake, and Paulo fetched a bottle of champagne. Ella grabbed at her fork as Mia took a bite of the delicious cake, savouring the explosion of sweetness in her mouth. 'Not for you, little one,' she said with a laugh as Ella's chubby fingers latched onto the fork.

'I'll take her.' With relaxed ease born now of experience, Alessandro reached for Ella, cradling her against his shoulder. As it always did, Mia's heart constricted at the sight of father and daughter, husband and child. Her family. A thrill ran through her at the thought, and one that had nothing to do with fear, and all with hope and even joy. This was real now. *They* were.

They ate cake and had champagne in the spring sunshine. Alessandro had planned a dinner for them, and Alyssa insisted on having Ella for the whole night, assuring Mia that the baby could sleep in her cottage.

'Ella is a good *bambina*,' Alyssa said firmly. 'She did not wake up even once. Such a good girl. This is your wedding night, Mia. Enjoy, Signora Costa!'

Signora Costa. Another ripple of surprised excitement shivered through her at the realisation of her new status.

The sun was starting to set, sending golden rays slanting through Mia's bedroom, as she exchanged her wedding gown for a cocktail dress in scarlet with a handkerchief hemline and a halter neck. Her wedding ring flashed as she did her make-up and hair, gazing at her face as if to look for changes. She was a married woman. And by tomorrow morning, she would *truly* be a married woman, in the way that mattered most…

Mia's stomach dipped as she considered the wedding night that loomed ahead of her, exciting and yet terrifying. Her one sexual experience had been short and frenzied, mere moments that had been blurred by passion.

Tonight would be in an entirely different category… and that both excited and scared her, with its promises of both pleasure and intense vulnerability. How would Alessandro be as a husband and lover? How would she be? Would she please him? Ella was only a few months old, and her body had changed since the last time he'd seen it, admittedly for only a brief time. What would he think of her gently rounded stomach, her heavier breasts?

A light knock sounded on the door. 'Ready, *cara*?' Alessandro called.

'I think so.' Mia gave her reflection one last tremulous glance before she went to the door and opened it. Alessandro stood there, looking as devastating as ever in a crisp button-down shirt in dove grey and darker grey trousers. He smelled wonderful.

'You look lovely,' he murmured, putting one hand on her waist as he pulled her to him for a prolonged kiss that made Mia's senses spin and reel. She wondered if kissing him would always make her blood fizz and her heart hum, or if it would become natural, even ordinary.

'So where are we going for dinner, exactly?' Mia asked as they headed downstairs. 'The trattoria in town?'

Alessandro chuckled, shaking his head. 'I think not.'

'There aren't any other restaurants…'

'This is our wedding night, Mia. We will celebrate in style.'

They walked out of the villa, and Mia stopped in surprise at the sight of the helicopter resting on the helipad in the distance, obscured by a few plane trees.

'Where…?'

'Come.' Taking her hand, Alessandro led her to the helicopter.

'But Ella…'

'We'll be back home in a few hours, never fear.' He helped her up into the helicopter as Mia's stomach fizzed with excitement. Where on earth was Alessandro taking her?

She found out an hour later, when they arrived in Venice, the city's many canals gleaming under the setting sun, the wedding-cake roof of San Marco Cathedral blazing with gold. Alessandro had hired out an entire restaurant by Piazza San Marco, the dining room flickering with candlelight, the canal mere steps away, the restaurant secluded and romantic as they were served course after course by a discreet waiter.

'This is amazing,' Mia breathed, in awe of the luxury and romance of it all.

The food was delicious, and she allowed herself a glass of champagne to celebrate, losing herself in the warm and unabashed admiration she saw in Alessandro's eyes. Tonight was made for magic.

And the magic continued as they walked hand in hand along the canal, chatting about everything and nothing. Alessandro had a dry sense of humour that made Mia laugh, and a sensitivity she hadn't expected, even though she'd seen it on display with their daughter. As they enjoyed the sights of the city of bridges, she felt as if her heart were a balloon inside her, filling up with hope, buoying higher and higher. Their marriage could work. Their marriage could even be amazing...

Finally, as twilight settled on the city with deep indigo shadows, the placid surface of the Grand Canal nearly black, they took the helicopter back to the villa.

Moonlight streamed through the windows as they walked quietly, still hand in hand, through the villa, up to the master bedroom Mia had been sleeping in alone for the last few weeks but would share with Alessandro tonight.

In the few hours since she'd been gone, it had been transformed: tall white candles flickered and gleamed, and the bed sheets had been exchanged for a silk duvet, folded back to reveal smooth linen sheets beneath. The nightgown of cobwebby lace and nearly transparent white silk that she'd picked out last week was hanging on the wardrobe door. Mia's heart tumbled in her chest at the sight of it.

'Is all this Alyssa's doing?' she asked.

'And mine.'

It thrilled her to think Alessandro had thought of such romantic touches. 'This is all so romantic...'

'And why shouldn't it be? It is our wedding night,

after all.' Alessandro stood behind her, his hands warm on her shoulders. 'It will be different this time, *cara*. So much better.'

Nerves fizzed and popped inside her. 'It was pretty good last time,' she admitted shakily. Now that the moment had come, and they were here together in this beautiful room, intending to consummate their marriage, she felt overwhelmed with both excitement and anxiety.

'Even so.' Alessandro nodded towards the nightgown. 'Do you want to change?'

'All right,' Mia whispered, and, taking the beautiful nightgown, she went into the bathroom.

Alessandro paced the bedroom, feeling restless and eager and, he had to admit, nervous. He was never nervous, and yet he couldn't deny the way his stomach clenched and his heart raced. Yes, he was nervous, but he was also excited. *Very* excited. He'd been waiting a long time for this, and more than once he'd questioned his decision to wait until their wedding night.

The evening had been perfect so far—the food and wine, the company, the romance of it all. Alessandro had never seen the point of such gestures before, but tonight they'd been important, and he'd enjoyed them. He'd wanted them. He'd wanted to make this night special for Mia, and special for him, in a way he'd never remotely wanted to before.

What was happening to him?

He thrust the question away, determined not to think about it tonight. This was just a bit of romance, that

was all. It was a way to show Mia he appreciated her.
It didn't have to mean anything more than that.

Besides, tonight he only wanted to think about Mia…
and what was going to happen between them.

The door to the bathroom opened and then she stood
there, her hair loose and golden about her shoulders, her
slender body swathed in ivory silk. Alessandro sucked
in a hard breath, dazed with desire at the sight of her.
The silk was so thin he could see the lush, shadowy
curves of her body beneath it, and they enflamed him.
The few rushed minutes they'd shared over a year ago
were nothing compared to this.

'You're still dressed,' Mia observed with a shaky
laugh.

'Not for long.' His hands moved to the buttons of his
shirt before they stilled. 'Why don't you do it, Mia?'

Her eyes widened. 'Me?'

'Yes, you.' His voice turned ragged with the force
of his feeling. 'I want you to. I want you to touch me.'

She stared at him wide-eyed for a few seconds before she moved towards him, the silk whispering against
her body. As she stood before him he breathed in her
citrusy scent, felt her hair brush his jaw as her fingers
fumbled with the first button.

'I'm nervous,' she whispered.

'So am I.'

She glanced up at him. 'No…'

'Yes.' He clasped her hand in his own and pressed it
against his thudding heart. 'Feel.'

She laid her palm flat against his chest, her fingers
spread wide. Even that simple touch enflamed him,

made him want more. So much more. 'Why are you nervous?'

'Because this feels important.' The words came of their own accord, heartfelt, honest. He didn't care what they revealed of him.

Mia glanced at him uncertainly, her hand still resting against his heart. 'You've been with plenty of women before…'

'Not like this. Never like this.'

'Truly?'

'Truly.'

She pressed her hand lightly against his chest, absorbing his words, the truth of them, and then she resumed unbuttoning his shirt. This time her fingers didn't fumble, and soon she was parting the material, sliding it over his shoulders so he was bare-chested.

'I never did get a good look at you before,' she remarked, her hands resting lightly on the sculpted muscles of his chest. His heart still thudded.

'You can look all you like now.'

'I am.' She ran her hand lightly down his chest, her fingers tracing the hard ridges of muscle, exploring his body in a way that made him feel dizzy with hunger for her even though her fingers were barely skimming his skin.

'Mia, you have no idea what you do to me.'

She ran her fingers along the waistband of his trousers before flicking open his belt as she gave him a mischievous look from under golden lashes. 'Don't I?'

He let out a choked laugh. 'Maybe you do, you imp.' He couldn't stand still any longer, submitting to her intoxicating touch. 'Now perhaps I need to discover what I do to you.' He put his hands on her arms, sliding them up to her shoulders, enjoying the feel of the silk of her skin, before he hooked one finger underneath the spaghetti strap of her nightgown and tugged it down.

Her breath came in a shudder and she swayed as he pressed a kiss to the pure line of her collarbone before moving lower to the soft swell of her breast.

'Alessandro…'

'It seems we affect each other in a similar way,' he murmured. Already he was blazing with need, on fire with it, and they'd barely touched.

'It does seem that way,' she admitted shakily. Her legs nearly buckled as he drew the other strap down, and then with one gentle twist of her shoulders the beautiful gown pooled at her feet, leaving her naked and beautiful. So very beautiful.

'I didn't wear that for very long,' she remarked with an attempt at wryness, although he could see the pulse beating wildly in her throat, her pupils dark and huge.

'It was in the way.'

'So are these.' She nodded towards his trousers, and Alessandro spread his hands.

'You may do the honours.'

With a gulp, she reached for the button, her fingers fumbling once more as she undid it and then started to tug down the zip, her slender fingers brushing the pulsing length of him, making him groan.

'Mia…' he began, and then he found he couldn't finish his sentence. He drew her into his arms, and in a tangle of naked limbs, he brought her to the bed and laid her on it like a treasure.

He kissed her deeply, drinking her in, feeling how her mouth and her whole body opened to him, an offering freely given—and utterly accepted.

He stretched out on top of her, relishing the feeling of her pressed against every inch of him, her arms wrapped around his shoulders, her breasts pressed to his chest, all his to explore and savour.

And he did, taking his time, coaxing an unfettered and glorious response out of Mia, his wife.

His wife.

The words, the truth of them, reverberated through him as he finally slid inside her welcoming warmth, uniting their bodies in a way they had never been united before, because this was for ever. One flesh, bound by a sacred vow.

For ever.

Mia's cry of pleasure was muffled against his shoulder as he began to move and she joined him, finding a rhythm they claimed for their own as it took them higher and higher, united in this, united in everything.

As one.

The realisation of it thudded through him in the aftermath of their joined explosion as Alessandro rolled onto his back, taking Mia with him. He never wanted to let her go.

He'd never expected this. All along he'd been planning his strategy, wooing his wife, poised for victory, negotiating the terms. She would be his.

He hadn't realised he would be hers.

But he felt it now in every sated fibre of his being, and this union between them that they had just consummated wasn't just special, it was sacred. It was overwhelming. And he knew, as he held her close, that he was in very grave danger of doing that which Mia herself had been so afraid of—losing himself. Giving everything to the woman he now held in his arms.

The woman who held his heart without even realising it. Without him ever having meant to give it to her.

CHAPTER FOURTEEN

IT HAS BEEN one month since she'd become Alessandro's wife, one amazing, incredible, pleasure-filled month. The days had been spent with Ella and often with Alessandro, when he could get away from work, spending time together in easy pleasures, exploring the market town and the surrounding countryside, and simply enjoying getting to know one another.

When Alessandro had to work at his office in Florence, Mia had pottered about the villa, taking over some of the duties from Alyssa, as well as learning Italian and attending a local mums and babies group. She'd been surprised how easy and pleasant it was to fill her days in this way, to simply enjoy being.

And as for her nights…those were filled as well, with a pleasure and intimacy she'd never expected or dared to dream of. Every night she and Alessandro explored each other's bodies, learning the maps of their very selves, and offering themselves to each other in a way that felt like the purest form of communication.

Each night left Mia both sated and shaken, as if she'd flown close to the sun, and been engulfed in its brilliance. It warmed her right through, but she also knew it had the danger to burn her right up.

Because, a month on from their marriage, she knew she was falling in love with her husband. She might have fought against it at the start, had worried all along that it would happen, and now she knew it was.

And she had no idea how her husband felt about her. At night she'd swear on her soul that he loved her, and he showed her he did in a thousand ways. But during the day...

Mia hadn't been able to fault him, at least not until recently. He'd been kind, affectionate, humorous, gentle with Ella. Yet all along she had never been able to escape the sense that he was still keeping some private yet essential part of himself from her. Whenever the conversation turned a little too personal, she felt a distance open up between them, a cool remoteness in Alessandro, as if he had picketed off part of himself and it absolutely wasn't up for grabs.

When she was alone, she told herself she must be imagining it. How on earth could she not be satisfied with all Alessandro gave her? It was such a vague notion, after all. Then, when they were together again, she felt it, like a part of her rubbed raw, always chafing. The words he'd never say, the sense that he wasn't hers, not in the way that she knew she was his. The remoteness was real...and it hurt.

And it had grown worse over the last few days, with Alessandro barely spending any time with her at all. He'd worked late, missing dinner as well as Ella's bedtime, coming to bed when Mia had already succumbed to a restless, unhappy sleep.

She hadn't asked him about his withdrawal; she hadn't, she acknowledged unhappily, been brave enough. Maybe he had some important deal at work. Maybe something else was going on.

But then, why couldn't he tell her about it?

And, more importantly, why couldn't she ask?

Now, with Ella settled in her bouncy chair as Mia prepared dinner, she could pretend, at least, they were just like any other family, any other loving couple. Alessandro had told her this morning he would be home for dinner, and hopefully they would sit and eat, talk and laugh, and everything so easy and simple…at least on the surface.

And when they went up to bed a little while later, it would be even simpler, because between the sheets Mia felt she had all of Alessandro to herself…body and soul.

There Alessandro never became a tiny bit repressive, a little tight-lipped. In bed, she never saw the flash of something in his eyes that reminded her of the man she'd met back in London, cold and autocratic, ruthless and remote. Not the man she married. Not the man she was beginning, to her own wonder and fear, to love.

Alyssa bustled into the kitchen, chucking Ella under her chin before turning to Mia. 'Something smells *molto delizioso*!'

Mia smiled wryly. 'I hope so. That is…*lo spero.*'

Alyssa beamed her approval. '*Molto buona!* Your lessons are coming on, *si*?'

'*Si.*' She'd been having several hours' tuition every day, and she hoped eventually to be fluent, to help Ella be fluent as well. Alessandro already talked to his daughter in Italian, something that made Mia melt inside. At moments like that, she could let herself believe in the fairy tale. She could be carried away by it.

'Is Signor Costa eating at home tonight?' Alyssa asked, and Mia nodded.

'Yes…that is, I hope so. *Lo spero.*' She smiled wryly again. 'He said he would before he left this morning.' Even though he hadn't for the few nights before, with no real explanation.

She was just setting the table, Ella bathed and gurgling in her bouncy chair, when her phone beeped with a text from Alessandro.

Working late.

Two measly words when she'd already prepared dinner, had everything ready. Mia's stomach swirled with disappointment and a far deeper hurt. This was the fourth night in a row. Feeling a bit reckless, she swiped her phone's screen to dial his number.

'Mia?' His voice was terse. 'Didn't you get my message?'

'Yes, but it's so late, Alessandro. I've already made dinner…'

'It will keep, won't it?'

Mia blinked at his brusque tone. No explanations, no apologies, just that edge of impatience to his voice, as if she was wasting his time.

'That's not the point, Alessandro,' she said, trying to keep her voice even. 'This is the fourth night you've missed dinner—'

'I'm working.' There was no mistaking the edge now. 'Surely you can understand that, Mia. I shouldn't have to justify it to you.'

'I'm not asking you to justify it,' she protested, startled by the definite coolness in his voice. 'Alessandro... what's going on?'

'What do you mean by that? Nothing is going on.'

'You've been so distant...'

'I'm *working*.'

Gone was even the pretence of the gentle, kind and attentive lover Mia had grown to know and love these last few weeks, making her wonder if it had all been a mirage.

'I know that,' she said quietly.

'Then there's no problem,' Alessandro answered, his voice clipped, and before Mia could say another word he disconnected the call.

She stood there for a moment, stunned by what had just happened, and yet somehow not surprised at all. Hadn't some part of her been waiting for this? For the mask to fall away, the true man to be revealed? All her fears to be realised?

She hadn't had the courage to confront Alessandro, and when she'd tried, he'd put her in her place, brushing off her concerns as if they were of no importance. The same way her father had.

It didn't have to be a big deal, Mia told herself. It was

one phone conversation. All couples had arguments. She was overreacting, she *knew* that. And yet…

But she knew it wasn't one conversation; it was everything that had and hadn't happened in the last month. On their wedding day—and night—she'd felt so wonderfully close to him, and the last month had been a sliding away from that, inch by infinitesimal inch.

Alessandro had been becoming more remote, and, worse, she had become more needy. More desperate. She'd heard it in her voice; she felt it in herself.

Drawing in a ragged breath, Mia reached for the pan of sauce simmering on the stove and recklessly she scraped it all into the bin.

She didn't want it to *keep*. Alessandro would most likely come home late tomorrow night as well. And the night after that…the night after that…

She couldn't live this way.

The realisation came suddenly, starkly, and was completely overwhelming, every fear she'd ever had rising restlessly to the fore. Here she was, just like her mother, miserable and alone, having just been told off by the man she was coming to love.

In her seat, Ella let out a happy gurgle, startling Mia out of her unhappy thoughts. She picked Ella up, pacing the kitchen, before she decided she couldn't stay in this villa for another moment. It felt like a mausoleum—a mausoleum of her fragile, fledgling hopes and dreams. As melodramatic as she knew that sounded, even in her own head, she also knew she needed some space.

Quickly Mia went upstairs and packed a case for both her and Ella. She needed to get out of here, get some perspective. And, she acknowledged, she wanted to show Alessandro that he wasn't the only one who could change plans.

It didn't take long to pack what she needed and ring a taxi. While waiting for the car to arrive, she'd checked out a family-friendly hotel in nearby Assisi. She'd go there for the night, she decided. Perhaps in the morning, things would feel and look better, and she'd know what to do. How to feel.

As the taxi sped away from the villa, Ella dozing in her car seat by her side, Mia glanced down at her phone. Alessandro hadn't called or texted again, but she knew he deserved at least some explanation as to her absence.

Needed to think, she texted,

And then waited for a reply that never came.

Alessandro glanced moodily at his phone. *Needed to think?* What was that supposed to mean? He hadn't bothered to reply, because he didn't know what to say. In truth, he hadn't known what to say for weeks now, as he fought the feeling that had been growing between them, stronger every day, and more alarming.

After the soul-changing encounter on their wedding night, when he'd realised just how far he'd fallen, he'd found himself inexorably withdrawing, trying to create a safe distance between him and Mia while pretending to her that it wasn't there.

It had been easy at night, when their bodies took over, and yet he knew that those earth-shattering nights were actually drawing them closer together. Making him want even more from Mia—and for her to want more than he was able to give.

Because during the day, when she asked about his family, or looked at him with so much expectation in her eyes, when he felt a welling of need inside him, a need that felt overwhelming and consuming…he started to freeze. To fear.

He was falling in love with Mia; hell, he was already in love with her, and he knew what happened when you loved someone. They rejected you. Eventually, always, they rejected you.

In his mind's eye he could see his mother's haggard face, the weary resignation in her face giving truth to her words.

'I wish I'd never had you.'

His own mother had wished him out of existence. His father hadn't wanted to know him at all. How on earth could he expect Mia to love him the way he knew he loved her…especially when she'd said she'd never wanted to love anyone at all? That had suited him admirably…once.

Now the only choice he felt he had was to keep himself safe. Separate. But the result was this restless ache, this impossible anxiety.

Needed to think?

He didn't like the sound of that at *all.*

Snatching up his phone and his coat, Alessandro decided he'd confront Mia directly, ask her just what she needed to think about. Even if he didn't like the answer, it was surely better to know.

It took an hour to drive back to the villa, and with

each minute Alessandro felt his insides coil tighter and tighter, till everything in him was ready to snap and break. What did Mia need to think about? What was going on?

He'd tell her he loved her, he decided recklessly. He'd admit the truth he'd been trying to hide from himself, even if the thought made his stomach cramp even more. Did he dare be that vulnerable? Open himself up to that much pain?

But what was the alternative? To live in this welter of frustration and fear, walking a tightrope between staying safe and being real? Gaining nothing or risking everything?

He'd always been willing to take a risk in business, and here was the biggest risk of all. He would be man enough to take it.

Filled with determination, powered by adrenalin, he drove up the sweeping lane to the villa, only to find it darkened and empty.

Perhaps she'd gone to bed already, he thought as he hurried upstairs.

'Mia…?' he called softly as he opened the door to their bedroom. It was empty, the bed still made up and untouched. Frowning, Alessandro walked down the hall to Ella's nursery, his blood freezing to ice in his veins at the sight of the empty cot, the open drawers, the missing clothes. Back to the master bedroom, and he saw that a suitcase was gone, along with some of Mia's clothes.

She'd left him, he realised hollowly. She'd actually left him. And she'd taken his daughter with him.

He sank onto the bed, caught between grief and rage.

So this was why Mia had needed to *think*? To think about whether she was leaving him—for a night, or perhaps, heaven help him, even for good? He couldn't see any other possibility. Memories of his childhood, of empty apartments, lonely nights and constant uncertainty, tormented him, and made him unable to think clearly, or even at all. All he knew was he was alone, and he hated it.

Alessandro dropped his head into his hands, overcome with emotion. Thank heaven he hadn't told her he loved her.

CHAPTER FIFTEEN

A NIGHT AWAY hadn't given Mia much rest. The hotel had been small and noisy, and Ella had had an unsettled night. Mia had, as well, missed the strong, solid presence of her husband in her bed. She'd gone away hoping to order her own thoughts, gain a bit of her independence back, but the time apart had only made her realise how much she missed Alessandro—and, yes, loved him.

The truth was stark and real, and she couldn't hide it from herself any longer. As she climbed in the taxi to head home the next morning, she let that realisation rest and then grow inside her, filling up all the empty space.

She loved him.

She hadn't meant to, hadn't wanted to, but she'd fallen in love with a man who most likely didn't feel the same way about her.

The realisation thudded dully inside her. This was the exact scenario she'd once feared, the one thing she'd never wanted to come to pass, and yet here she was, knowing it was true and having to deal with it.

How?

By telling Alessandro she loved him? The thought filled Mia with frightened panic, and yet she also knew, intrinsically and instinctively, that it was the right thing to do. What kind of love was it if she couldn't even admit to it? And if he was horrified, if he told her flat out he didn't love her back...well, then at least she'd know.

As the taxi came up the villa's drive, hope warred with icy terror. Could she really do this? What if, improbably, impossibly, Alessandro told her he loved her back? Dared she even dream...?

Mia held on to that hope as she climbed out of the taxi, Ella in her arms. She'd just paid the driver and started towards the steps when the front door was thrown open.

'Where the *hell* have you been?'

Mia froze at the sound of Alessandro's condemning voice, the cold rage she heard in it, as he strode towards her, everything about his taut form and angry voice catapulting her back to her childhood.

'I told you...' she began, faltering at the sight of the thunderous look on her husband's face.

'You told me you needed to *think*! And then I came home to an empty house, no explanation, my daughter *gone*...'

'I went away for a night, that's all...'

'Without telling me so. Without telling me where.' Alessandro shook his head, his eyes dark, his lips compressed. 'How could you, Mia? How could you do such a thing?' He shook his head again before she could form a reply. 'I don't care. No reason is good enough.'

'Then I won't bother giving you one,' Mia snapped, goaded into her own rage by his high-handed manner. To think she'd been about to tell him she loved him! 'It seems you can come and go as you please, but I can't.'

'That's completely different. I was working.'

'While I was playing with the fairies? Never mind.' Anger and hurt choked her voice. 'I don't care. I'm going inside.' She pushed past him, only to have him reach for her arm.

'Mia—'

'Leave me alone.' She shrugged off his hand, her eyes blinded by tears, and hurried inside. It was, she realised as she headed upstairs, the first argument they'd had since they'd been married, and it felt as if it might be the last one as well. How had everything gone so disastrously wrong so quickly? Except it hadn't been quick at all. It had been happening all month. This was just the result.

Ella was fussing, so Mia fed and changed her before putting her down for a nap. Then she had a shower, hoping it might make her feel better, but everything only made her feel worse. She thought of going in search of Alessandro, but couldn't bear the thought of another argument, or, worse, a freezing silence.

How had it got this bad between them? Was there any way to make it better?

'Mia.' Alessandro stood in the doorway of the bedroom as she came out of the bathroom, finger-combing her damp hair. She stilled as she saw him, everything in her poised for flight.

'What is it?' she asked warily.

He shook his head slowly. 'I've been thinking.'

That didn't sound good. 'Thinking? About what?'

'About us.'

Her hands stilled and she turned to face him fully, lowering her hands from her hair. 'Alessandro…?'

'I never gave you a choice, Mia.'

What…?

'You did,' she protested, scanning his face for clues to what he was feeling.

'Not really. I as good as sent you to California, and then I took you from there, without you being able to do much about it. I practically forced you to marry me…'

Mia gazed at him, trying to figure out where he was going with this. 'But you asked me to choose, Alessandro. I was the one who proposed, after all—'

'Do you really think that was any choice at all? If you'd said no, I would have seduced you. I would have had my way. I was always determined about that. There was absolutely no way you weren't going to marry me, Mia.' He met her gaze bleakly, and Mia shook her head.

'Why are you telling me this now?'

'Because I realise I can't do this any more. I can't give you what you need, what you deserve.'

'Which is what?' Mia whispered.

'Love.' He spoke the word flatly. 'It's too hard for me, Mia. With my childhood…my parents… I can't do it.'

'Did I ever say I wanted you to love me?' Mia asked in a shaking voice, even though it hurt to say the words, because in her heart and mind she'd been asking him, begging him every day. Had he been able to see that? Had it horrified him?

'A marriage needs love as its foundation,' Alessandro stated. 'Without it, it will always crumble at one point or another. It won't be strong enough to endure. I've realised that now…and I realise that what we have isn't enough.'

'So what are you really saying?' Mia asked, her voice hardening. 'You want a divorce?'

'We could probably arrange an annulment, or otherwise, yes, a quiet divorce.'

'And what about Ella?' Mia demanded, her voice catching on her daughter's name. 'What about her needing a father? You insisted on that—'

'We'll arrange visits. I can still be part of her life. I want to be. That won't change.'

'Visits.' Mia felt faint suddenly, her vision blurring, as the awful import of everything Alessandro was saying slammed into her. Slowly she walked to the bed and sank onto its edge, blinking the world back into focus. 'Why are you telling me this now? Is it because of our argument? What made you realise all this so suddenly?' Her voice rose and then broke. 'Was none of this real?'

'How could it have been?' Alessandro returned rawly. 'Considering?'

Tears stung her eyes then and she did her best to blink them back. She felt as if her heart was being wrung like a rag inside her, squeezing out its last painful drops of love. 'So all this time, you've just been pretending? Orchestrating a takeover? You are known to be subtle,' she added bitterly. 'Even when it's hostile.'

'Don't think of it like that, Mia…'

'How am I supposed to think of it?' she demanded. 'Either our marriage was real or it wasn't. Either the vows you made were sacred and binding or they weren't.'

'I'm trying to be fair and give you your freedom—'

'Some freedom. What am I supposed to do now?'

He spread his hands. 'Whatever you want. I'll make sure you have a generous settlement. You'll want for nothing—'

'I'll want for everything.' Mia's voice broke. 'Why are you doing this, Alessandro?'

'Because I told you, I realised that a marriage needs more than what we have to grow—'

'And you're so sure you can never, ever love me? Learn to love me, if it's so important?' Her voice broke as the full force of rejection hit her. He stayed silent, and she looked up, and for the first time she saw the torment on his face. 'Or are you worried that I can't love you?' she whispered, barely daring to say the words. 'Is that what this is about, Alessandro? Are you afraid?'

'I'm not afraid.'

'Then say the words,' she demanded. 'Say, "Mia, I don't love you and I never will."' He stayed silent and she rose, her hands balled into fists by her sides, risking everything on this. '*Say* them.'

'Mia…' He stopped and shook his head. 'I don't want to hurt you.'

'Well, you're failing miserably at that, because you already have. Immeasurably. And what I think, Alessandro, is that *you* don't want to be hurt. So tell me now that you don't love me. Make it real.'

He sighed heavily, his gaze averted. 'I'm not sure I know how to love.'

'So…'

A hesitation, endless, awful, as he searched her face, steeling himself. 'No,' Alessandro said finally. 'I don't love you. I… I never will.'

Mia had been bracing herself for it, expecting it, but those two simple, stark words still held the power to fell her. She swayed where she sat and two tears slipped quickly and coldly down her cheeks before she could stop them. She dashed her eyes with the back of her arm and then stood up on wobbly legs.

'Fine. I'll pack in the morning.'

'It's better this way…'

No, it wasn't. It wasn't at all. But at least she knew now. With a leaden heart, Mia walked out of the bedroom—and away from her husband.

He was a coward. Alessandro lay in bed, gritty-eyed as he stared at the ceiling. Mia was sleeping in a guest bedroom, and he missed her presence with a ferocity that undid him…but even more overwhelming and shaming was the truth pounding through him that he hadn't been brave enough to admit.

I don't love you.

Except he did. Of course he did. And in the moment she'd asked he'd known what a pathetic coward he was, because he'd been afraid to admit it. The most crucial moment of his life, and he'd blown it out of fear. He'd lied, because it had seemed easier. It had felt safer. Because letting her walk away now was surely better than letting her hurt him later…or, heaven forbid, hurting her.

Except he'd just hurt her unbearably.

I don't love you. The cruellest words he could have said, as terrible as the words his mother had said to him, which had tormented him for decades. How could he have done it? How could he have let himself?

It would have been worse later, he told himself for the tenth time. *Surely it would have been worse later.*

Except right now it felt like hell.

He shifted in the bed, knowing sleep would never come. Would she really leave in the morning, with Ella? Had he just fractured his family, and for what purpose? He'd convinced himself he'd been noble, saving her from a loveless marriage. How deluded was he, thinking that was the right choice? Mia had seen through him, of course. She'd known what this was really about.

It wasn't about him not loving her…it was about him loving her too much. It was about how loving someone meant losing yourself, just as they'd both feared, in their own ways. And gaining so much more…if Mia loved him back.

Why was he so scared to risk it? Risk himself? Could this really, possibly, be better?

It had to be.

The next morning, after a sleepless night, Alessandro came downstairs to find Mia already packed, Ella in her arms.

'You're going already…' Even though he'd been expecting it, he could scarcely believe the sight in front of him.

'It seems better.' Mia's voice was flat, her shoulders slumped. She looked as if all the life had drained out of her, as if the very will to live had been sucked from her soul.

He'd done this, Alessandro realised. This was his fault. This was all going so horribly wrong, simply because he hadn't had the courage to take the biggest risk you could in this life…loving someone else. Giving them your heart. Accepting theirs in return.

And he knew he couldn't let it end this way. He wouldn't. He wouldn't live life as a coward, unwilling to take the biggest risk of all, to let go of control and hand someone his heart. 'Mia, wait.'

She looked at him with lifeless eyes, Ella clutched in her arms. 'Do you love me?' he asked, the words raw, his voice quavering.

She stared at him blankly, her face so weary and sad, tears nearly stung his eyes. 'Why are you asking that now, Alessandro?'

'Because…because it's important. Because I should have asked last night, when you asked me.'

'Why do you care, when you've already told me how you feel?' Mia responded quietly. 'Do you just want to pour salt into my wound? Isn't it enough that you don't love me?'

He hesitated, poised to fly, afraid to fall. Even now, with everything at stake, he held back. And in his silence was his condemnation.

'I've called a taxi,' Mia said. 'It should be here now.'

Alessandro glanced at her one small travel bag. 'Where are your bags?'

'I'm leaving everything here. I… I don't want it. I certainly don't need all those fancy gowns and things.' From outside they heard the crunch of tyres on gravel. Mia hoisted her bag in one hand, Ella in her car seat in the other.

This was it. The end. She was really leaving, because he was going to let her.

Do you love me?

She hadn't answered the question, and Alessandro couldn't blame her, considering what his own response had been last night.

He'd said he wasn't capable of love, or even that he knew what it was, and yet…what if he did?

What if in this moment he really did?

What if real love wasn't a safe landing, but a dangerous fall? What if it was risking everything, not knowing the result? Letting yourself get hurt, because that was part of the whole, terrifying, incredible deal?

Mia was at the door, one hand reaching for the handle, the seconds sliding past far too fast.

'Mia!' His voice came out in a shout of command that made her stiffen. 'Mia,' he said more softly. 'Please wait.'

'Why? What is there left to say?'

He swallowed hard, his throat impossibly tight. Now. He needed to say it now. She reached for the handle again.

'I love you.'

The words fell into the stillness, and even now part of him wanted to snatch them back. The last time he'd said them had been to his mother, and she'd wearily told him she wished she'd never had him. He'd vowed never to say them again. Never to want or need to say them again.

But Mia had changed him. Loving Mia had changed him.

'Alessandro…' She shook her head slowly. 'Why are you saying this now? You can't mean it…'

'I do. I was too much of a coward to say it before. But the truth is I've been falling in love with you for months now, and fighting it all the way.' His words came faster and more assuredly, and the release of finally being open and honest was strangely wonderful. Freeing in a way he'd never expected. 'I never wanted to love anyone, Mia. My mother didn't love me, and I wanted her to, desperately. She told me she wished she'd never had me…she forgot about and neglected me time and again, and still I wished she'd love me. I loved her.' He swallowed hard, the words coming faster and faster as he tried to explain. 'At a young age I told myself I'd never let someone have that kind of control over me. I'd be the one who was in control, always, and I made that my life's mission. Yet here I am, risking everything because it's too important not to. Because I love you too much, and I don't want to be a coward any more. I love you, Mia. I love you.'

He spread his hands wide, his heart thudding as he waited for her response.

'You…love me?' She sounded incredulous as she turned from the door and put down her bag and Ella's car seat.

'With all my soul. All my heart. I'm terrified, Mia.

I'm shaking.' He let out a ragged laugh. 'And yet here I am, giving everything I have to you. You can do with it as you will. You can walk out that door as you were intending to, or you can come over here and slap my face and tell me what an arrogant imbecile I am.' He took a quick, steadying breath. 'Or you can tell me you love me back, or even that you could learn to love me, like you asked me to last night, and you'll give us a chance even though I've been so very stupid and scared. I wasn't giving you your freedom… I was trying to find mine. I'm sorry. I don't want you to go. I love you.'

He was babbling, but he didn't care. He'd say anything to make her stay…even, *especially*, the truth.

'I've been afraid too,' Mia said after a long moment. 'I've been fighting it too, because I was scared of losing myself, like I said. So scared, and yet it happened anyway.'

'Yes.' Alessandro's voice was fervent. 'But I realised last night that loving someone means losing yourself—to another person. Entrusting them with everything that you are. And that's terrifying, but it's also so good and right. I know I'll mess up, Mia, so many times. I'll be angry or thoughtless or bossy or… something. But I'll try. And I hope you'll forgive me. And learn to love—'

'Oh, Alessandro, you idiot,' Mia said with tears in her voice. 'I already love you. I've loved you for ages. I just thought you'd never love me. You'd never do what you just said, and offer me everything. Ever since our wedding I've felt you've been holding something back…'

'I know. I have been. But it's yours now. All of it—me—is yours. I'll tell you whatever you like. I'll give you the parts of myself I've been trying to hide, the ones that are dark and ugly and needy. And hopefully you won't be put off—'

'Never,' Mia whispered. Tears trickled down her face, and with a jolt Alessandro realised he was crying too.

'So you'll stay?'

'Yes.' Mia walked towards him, her arms held out, so all it took were two steps for Alessandro to catch her up in his, pulling her body closely to his. Home. He was home. 'I'll stay,' Mia whispered as he lowered his head to kiss her. 'I'll stay. For ever.'

EPILOGUE

Three years later

SUN BEAMED DOWN on the terrace as Mia stepped out, baby Milo in her arms. It was her son's christening, three months after his birth. Just like Ella, he had Alessandro's grey eyes and her blonde hair. He gurgled up at her now before catching sight of his father and reaching out chubby arms to him.

'Hello, *caro*,' Alessandro said, scooping up his son easily and planting a kiss on his plump cheek. 'It's your special day.'

'She's been good as gold,' Alyssa said as she joined them on the terrace, holding Ella, now three and a half, by the hand. 'A very proud big sister.'

Mia smiled at Ella, and then shared a loving look with Alessandro. The last three years had been so wonderful, so blessed. Admittedly, it hadn't always been easy. They'd had their battles and struggles, both of them learning day by day to let go of control, of their very selves, as they committed themselves to each other in small yet significant ways.

Now Alessandro brushed a kiss across her lips as he cradled their son. 'Happy?' he asked softly, his eyes full of warmth and tenderness that, even after three years, made Mia melt inside.

She reached for his free hand, lacing her fingers through his. 'Yes,' she told him, thankful for so much, and especially this man by her side who had chosen to share his life, his very self, with her. 'Very, very happy.'

* * * * *

Captivated by Kate Hewitt's
The Italian's Unexpected Baby?
You won't be able to resist these other
Secret Heirs of Billionaires stories!

Sheikh's Royal Baby Revelation
by Annie West

Cinderella's Scandalous Secret
by Melanie Milburne

Unwrapping the Innocent's Secret
by Caitlin Crews

Proof of Their One-Night Passion
by Louise Fuller

Available now!

WE HOPE YOU
ENJOYED THIS BOOK!

HARLEQUIN™

Presents®

Get lost in a world of international luxury, where billionaires and royals are sure to satisfy your every fantasy.

Discover eight new books every month, available wherever books are sold!

HPHALO2019

#3789 BOUND BY MY SCANDALOUS PREGNANCY
The Notorious Greek Billionaires
by Maya Blake

Two months ago, I stood outside Neo's office ready to beg forgiveness. Instead, I found myself begging for more, as he set me ablaze with his touch. Now I must tell him I'm pregnant with the child he never expected!

#3790 CROWNED AT THE DESERT KING'S COMMAND
by Jackie Ashenden

The borders of Tariq's kingdom are closed—just like his ironclad heart. After rescuing lost archaeologist Charlotte from the desert, he *can't* let her go. Instead, their mutual desire compels Tariq to crown Charlotte as his queen!

#3791 CRAVING HIS FORBIDDEN INNOCENT
by Louise Fuller

Basa may have almost succumbed to their heated attraction once, but after Mimi's criminal family almost ruined his own, he *won't* be fooled twice. But, thrown together for a society wedding, Basa's fierce control is threatened by her forbidden temptation...

#3792 REDEMPTION OF THE UNTAMED ITALIAN
by Clare Connelly

Cesare is sure one sinful encounter with Jemima will be enough. It's not! Nothing less than claiming her for a red-hot fling will do. But to unravel Jemima's secrets, the Italian must first prove himself worthy of her...

HPCNMRB0120